The Housekeeper

ALSO BY SADIE RYAN

STANDALONES
The Proposal
The Secretary
The Housekeeper

THE HOUSEKEEPER

SADIE RYAN

Choc Lit

A JOFFE BOOKS COMPANY

Revised edition 2024
Choc Lit
A Joffe Books company
www.choc-lit.com

First published as *Guilty* in Great Britain in 2021

Cover art by Nick Castle

ISBN: 978-1781898154

CHAPTER 1

Lindy

My name is Linda Villas or Lindy; I like Lindy. Most of my friends, not that I have any left, call me Lindy. I'm from Charlottesville, Virginia. And I want to murder my husband.

Of all the screwed-up people out there, I'm probably one of the worst. I know it, I don't need anyone to diagnose me, that's already been done for the record. Like other unstable people I had my tipping point, which came a year ago — that's what they told me at the hospital. At least, I hope it did, I don't think I was unstable before. Who knows. We can all be unstable; it only takes something to tip the scales.

My noticeable southern accent, which the Brits love but which in the States is less of an attribute, attracts unwanted attention. I'm sat in a pub right now nursing a glass of wine. It's my second while I wait for Mia.

She's late, which is unusual for her. Her timing is impeccable, unlike mine. We don't live that far apart though she doesn't know that. I used to live at the back of her before we had to sell our house.

1

Mia is always polite and friendly, although I doubt she remembers me from one encounter to the next. Surprising really; while I'm not beautiful like her, I thought I might have made an impression by being the opposite. I don't think Mia thinks mean things about people. Something about her tells me she's not cruel. Don't ask me why I'm fixated on her, I just am. I find her fascinating and, well, I've got into a habit of watching her.

I've lived in the UK for thirty years. I married a Brit whom I met while vacationing over here and then moved here for love. That's right, head over heels love. I was seeing the world through rose-tinted glasses, you know how it is when you fall in love — you go a little gaga. Everything in my world was peachy at the time, like the universe was trying to fulfil all my dreams. What could go wrong when everything was going so right? Right?

I was so excited when I met my husband, like I'd found the golden chalice. Nobody had ever been in love like me, Lindy Villas, I thought. I wonder now how I would have reacted if I had known that the man of my dreams would turn out to be the man of my nightmares. I would have died for Frank. You see, I'd met my other half. My soulmate. I suppose we all get swept up in love sometime or another. We were smug in our love. We'd smile at couples arguing. Sitting in restaurants, cafés or on park benches with nothing to say to each other. Pitying the poor saps that never felt the power of love.

When that love crashes and burns, boy is that a long way to fall. Falling isn't the problem as much as the landing. Hitting the deck. Smashing into concrete headfirst. That's what it feels like when your life loses trajectory. When the unexpected bump in the road is a ruddy great cavernous hole that you fall into.

My kids are all grown up — twenty-five and twenty. I had my babies when I was very young. The joy, the love. It was all I could think of when I found out I was pregnant, the unbelievable idea of a life growing inside me was overwhelming. Each stage of their development was total fulfilment. I never wanted them to grow up. Some people can't wait for them to grow up. To become self-sufficient. Not me. I loved their dependency on me. I adored that. I was their whole universe, like they were mine. They still are. I love being a mum. Bringing up my kids was the happiest time of my life. That bond a mom has is indestructible — tangible too, like an invisible umbilical cord that never snaps. That reaches across time and space, pulling you back again and again.

Mia has two children the same age. I take a drink of my wine and think of her. It's not difficult to find out about a person these days. In fact, it's remarkably easy. Less irksome than I thought. I don't have friends anymore; I think I mentioned that, not after what happened. It doesn't bother me, the lack of friends, sometimes it's better. Less stressful. Mia is someone I sort of met. Meaning I kind of fabricated a meet cute. Not out of love, but from obsession.

We're not friends as such right now. But we will be soon. It's just a matter of convincing her. It's a gut feeling. Some people don't believe in gut feelings. I was one of them once. I should have listened to mine but of course I didn't. Hindsight. Hindsight. Hindsight. My God, how much better off we'd all be with a little hindsight. Well, for starters, I would not be here drinking like some poor loner. Obsessing over Mia. And wanting to kill my husband. Well, we all have our choices. And I've made mine.

I should have listened that night. I should have trusted what I felt. But I foolishly thought I was over-reacting. I didn't want an argument. I didn't want a fight. I should have trusted ME. Now all I have are nightmares.

After it happened I was catatonic. I spent some time in one of those charming hospitals where they handle you as if you're made of paper. They gave me lovely pills that stopped the nightmares and sat me in a cheerless room with other flimsy people.

I didn't speak for a long time. For four months I didn't utter one single word. Living like that was peaceful. Then they took the nice pills away from me, one at a time, which made me angry, aggressive, and paranoid. You see, without the pills the terrible nightmares came back.

Frank wanted to take me home. He told the nice doctors he would look after me, but I didn't want to live with Frank. Not anymore. But there was no one else to look after me. I couldn't blame them. Who'd want me in their house? Officially, I now have a mental illness and its label is anxiety.

Do you know anxiety comes in many forms? I didn't. I didn't even know I had it until they told me. 'Mrs Villas, you are suffering from anxiety brought on by trauma. Many who suffer don't display signs on the outside that anything is wrong. Like an iceberg, all lovely up top but beneath the surface, they're struggling.' He had a way with words, did my doctor.

I never suffered from anxiety before that day. That. Day. That God awful fucking day.

I clear the lump in my throat and blow my nose. You see, I was always a cup half-full type of girl. Now, I'm half empty. I catch a glimpse of myself in the mirrored back of the bar and think how I lock myself away inside my mind most of the time with all its unclean thoughts and wonder if anyone can read them. It's irrational, I know. I can't help it. I try fighting it and push myself forward. Push myself through the dank miasma that is now my life.

Frank knows when I'm bad and keeps out of my way. Normally I keep out of his too, because it's at these times when the nightmares, visions, and memories come alive and I can't deal with them. I know when it's coming. Hijacking me. Squeezing my chest like an accordion. Pushing out all the air and pressing my lungs and heart flat. The pain in my chest is crippling, but nothing is worse than the visions. You can't run away from your thoughts. They're everywhere you turn.

People who know us avoid us. I catch them looking at me in the street or the shops and I detest it. Their sad little faces.

Faces I want to shove into a paper shredder. I've seen that look too many times. I hate their pity, it makes my insides twist.

It's not the anxiety that has driven me to want to murder Frank. It's him. 'I'm sorry, Lindy. I'm so sorry. I should have listened to you. I'm in pain too.' Frank's words creep over me like a flesh-eating virus. I turn my phone over and check the time. Mia is ridiculously late today, so unlike her. A stupid urge grips me, to call the gym where she works and check if she's left. I decide against it. Maybe she's not coming tonight. I glance in the mirror again and see her friends. Drinking. Laughing. She must be on her way, though; they all look as if they're waiting for her.

Frank and I live in Chelford. It's a small village in Cheshire about twenty miles south of Manchester. In the beginning we lived in a charming what you Brits call *bijou cottage*. It was small and compact and all we could afford at the time. Nestled in the corner of the village with a yard in the back big enough for some pots and the trash. We were in love and who the heck cares when you're in love. When we arrived, we were full of unbridled enthusiasm, eager to start our new life together. As soon as we opened the door, it burst like a dam.

We rushed in and stopped dead. It was the smell. It was so different to what we remembered now it was empty. It was smaller. Lots smaller. We stared at the walls, now bare of pictures, at the ugly outline they'd left behind. The warm yellow of the walls that had looked so cosy when we'd come to view was nicotine, we now realised. It reeked. The scent of vanilla that I remembered must have come from air fresheners and scented candles. There had been cooking smells, baking and fresh coffee. All of which I now appreciated had been concocted to cover the terrible stomach-churning smell of old tobacco.

We laughed and ran upstairs. We made love quickly and passionately in the bedroom, Frank threw down his coat on the hideous multicoloured carpet. Over the moving in period we made love in every room, even the kitchen. It was uncomfortable and awkward in such a tight space but we were young

5

and it was all a great adventure. Everything was a great adventure then.

The bedrooms were small too. No king-size bed would fit, no wardrobes. The stairs were narrow, the bend in them too tight. We didn't care. We made love everywhere. Who needed a king-sized bed? We wanted to be close. Together. In each other's arms as much as possible. The peach-coloured bathroom needed ripping out but we knew that already. Who cared? Not us. We bathed together every day. We were in love and that's what couples in love did. There wasn't a shower. Did we care? The cottage was old, the wooden doorways were low and Frank had to stoop to get through them. 'How did we not notice this?' he said, grinning like a loon as he bumped his head, again.

'I've no idea. It's like a different house altogether.' The banister was rickety. Only one person at a time fitted in the dingy kitchen. It was a great excuse not to cook. We ate out a lot anyway, as young couples do. When you're young and in love you feel you can overcome anything. Nothing is too much trouble. 'There are no problems, only solutions,' we used to say.

Over the years we extended out and up, making it into a less bijou and more spacious family home. We made it open plan with a large kitchen diner. We built a conservatory on the back and Frank turned the garden into an oasis of colour and tranquillity. We've sold our charming cottage now. We had to move. Now we live at the back of Mia. I love that I live so close to her. She's married to Ricky. Did I say?

If love makes you do crazy, stupid things, what does falling out of love make you do? Crazier, stupider things?

'Bartender, I'll have another of the same, please.'

The pub is across from the gym. I've eaten here a few times when I've not wanted to go home. I have to admit the food isn't bad, it's one of those gastro pubs. I usually have the fish and chips and mushy peas and people watch. It's one of my favourite British meals.

It's been recently refurbished into an upbeat, contemporary eatery. The Dirty Fox. I like the name. It could apply to most of the regulars who come here straight from work. At 6 p.m. the bar is lined with a skulk of silver foxes, their eyes on the young singletons or recently divorced/widowed vixens. I don't include myself in that category, just so you know. Probably about half of the silver foxes have vixens at home. Dirty dogs.

Mia works as a personal trainer at the gym. Real name Michelle Hicks. Ricky is always very attentive. He's her husband, the old-fashioned kind of guy that comes and picks her up after a night out. I guess she's too precious to get in a taxi — you never know what might happen in this day and age. She comes from a good home. Her uncomplicated parents that have done very well for themselves live on the edges of Knutsford in a large Victorian house. A couple of sisters that live their lives out on Facebook. There's really no need for me to shine a light on how different we are to each other. But we're connected, I can feel it.

My fixation on Mia started recently. She helped me in the supermarket car park. My bag for life burst, shedding all my shopping. She came to help. There was something about her delicate femininity that day that caught my attention.

After that I kept seeing her, bumping into her in different shops. The café, the chemist. The park where she walked her dogs and I walked with the demons inside my head. I've wondered if the universe was trying to align us. When you start dipping your toe in those murky waters dangerous thoughts rise to the surface. We never chatted on those occasions, we acknowledged each other with a wave and a smile. Then I found myself looking out for her all over town. Following her. Stalking her.

I should have stopped then. I should have known this was going to lead to dangerous ground. Maybe I should have been more aware of what was happening to me, to my fogged-up brain. Too many "should haves". Besides, I didn't want to look too deep inside myself. Too ugly in there.

'Thanks,' I say to the bartender and smile as he hands me my glass of medium Chablis that's taken him an age to deliver. He's too busy on his phone. Probably on Tinder. I drink nothing but Chablis. It's pretentious, I know, but who gives a fig.

It's pretty much the only thing I treat myself to anymore, and it helps. As the cool liquid slides down my throat, thoughts of how ugly I am inside slip from my mind.

He smiles back but if Mia were here, he'd hang around and try to start up a flirty conversation. I don't want to think of him panting after Mia like a dog on heat.

'Quiet in here this evening, isn't it?' I say, to see if he'll flirt with me.

'That's Monday nights for you,' he replies without looking up from his phone. It was what I expected but I like to keep trying. Vanity, I guess. I don't have much of that anymore. Occasionally it flares up, like hives.

I don't much like to interact with people or the world in general. That's not how I was. It is how I am now. Solitude brings its own pain. Like your thoughts. When there's nothing else to distract you, all you have are your thoughts, crashing into each other like a slow-motion pile-up on some motorway. Over and over and over. The cracks in my life are cavernous. Most days navigating them is straightforward. Other days it's as if the ground beneath my feet opens up into huge gaping fissures waiting to drag me down.

I'm tired. Done in. Weary, I rest my elbow on the bar and my head in my hand. I hardly register the noise coming from Mia's waiting friends. The wine is lulling me into a comfortable, cotton wool blanket.

Once again I check my phone for the time. I'll be pissed by the time Mia arrives; she's forty-five minutes late now. I know I drink too much. I don't care what you think. It helps. They tell me it doesn't. *They*, the ones who think they can help me. LOL, as my girls would say.

A woman at the other end of the bar smiles at me. I don't smile back. Why is she smiling? I don't know her. Then I see the pity and turn my tear-filled eyes away. The lump in my throat threatens to asphyxiate me. I blink several times and wait for the tightness to ease before drinking at least half my glass of wine.

Frank won't pick me up; I'll have to grab a taxi. Mia's always in here by 7.30 p.m. on a Monday. The bartender slides over a dish of salted peanuts, it clinks against the stem of my glass. Yeah, wise guy, I know your trick, coax me to consume those suckers and I'll be ordering another glass of your massively expensive Chablis. Do I look as if I'm twenty? Besides, who in their right mind eats peanuts in a bar? I dread to think of the unwashed fingers that have dipped into that pot. Those men. All those guys who don't wash their hands when they've taken a leak. I slide the dish back down the bar. Mia's friends are getting louder and drunker.

'Sorry, I couldn't get away.' Mia makes her entrance through the front door, like the Queen of Sheba. Heads turn in her direction and the bartender straightens up like he's had a rod shoved up his backside. Mia has eyes only for her friends.

There's always a slight edge to Mia that I can't quite put my finger on. I've wondered on occasion if there might be something amiss in what looks like her perfect life.

'The class was late starting because a woman fell off the bike and we had to call an ambulance and then she was worried about her kids and the babysitter, so I called them for her.' She's talking quickly and loudly, checking her phone as she walks towards her friends.

The loop of music playing through the music system starts over — Ed Sheeran again. I sigh. 'Hey!' I call out to the bartender who is fixated on Mia. He glances in my direction, annoyed. 'Have you nothing else to play but this guy?' I point to the speaker above our heads. 'Or are you paying homage to the man tonight? I'm sick of listening to this crappy sentimental bullshit.' He shrugs and turns away.

'Christ, Mia, was she pedalling that fast?' one of them asks. Sitting at the bar with my Chablis, I have a mental image of limbs speeding like pistons.

Mia laughs, a tinkling sound like ripples on a still pond. 'She hadn't even started. She landed on her right hand, poor thing. The paramedics said she broke her wrist.' She picks up an empty bottle of wine and shakes it. 'I think I have a bit of catching up to do.' She checks the time on her phone. Sends a quick text then drops it into her handbag, furrowing her brow. Pulling it out again and reading the text a second time. What could be wrong in Mia's world that could possibly cause such a frown?

'Hey, let's get a couple more bottles,' someone says.

I catch the bartender's eye and call him over before he can serve them, but Mia is suddenly standing next to me and his attention is all on her: 'Hey there, what can I get for you?' His slimy tone makes me cringe. Does he think he's Joey out of *Friends*? I want to say that I called him first, but what's the point, I'm totally invisible right now. I drink my wine and watch the scene from over the rim of my glass. She looks nervous and keeps checking her phone. She hasn't noticed me perched on the bar stool slightly inebriated. Must be my new haircut. I remember when I used to look that good. My business power suit, the sleek hair and makeup. That woman seems like someone I knew in the distant past. I can hardly picture her.

She smiles back at the bartender and lifts her hair off her neck, as if to cool off. It doesn't quite come off the same way when I do it. She's still in gym clothes and looks amazing. 'Can I get a couple of bottles of red wine, please?' She points to the table with her girlfriends. 'Can you put it on that tab?' Her voice is sensual. Husky. It strikes him dumb for a few seconds.

The bartender blinks and smiles, showing his white capped teeth. Straightens his shoulders and pushes out his chest. What a peacock. He puts two bottles of red on a tray. 'I'll carry them over for you.'

I try catching his attention but there's no chance. 'Excuse me,' I say, lifting my hair off my neck like Mia. He ignores me a second time. I sigh. Drink. What's the point?

'Are you ladies going to be eating with us?' He asks, almost devouring Mia with his eyes. "*You ladies*" doesn't include me, of course. He means, is Mia eating here. I have an urge to roll his tongue back into his mouth before it knocks her bottles of wine off the tray.

Mia grabs the tray. 'I can manage these, thanks. The lady would like serving.' She inclines her head in my direction and I see her trying to remember where she knows me from. The bartender looks at me like he's seeing me for the first time. Prick. I give him my best Mr Spock eyebrow.

I smile gratefully at Mia. 'How are you?' I ask, hoping she might remember me.

Then she twigs. 'Sorry, I didn't recognise you. Have you done something to your hair?'

I smooth it down, as if I'd forgotten. 'Oh, yes. I had it cut. Thought it would help.' Another roll of the eyes. I'm not sure why I keep rolling my eyes, it's giving me a headache. It's because I'm a little drunk. I should stop drinking before I say something inappropriate. Not that I care that much if I do.

'Great,' she says, looking confused. 'How're you keeping? Hair looks good by the way.' She adds it as if it's what she's supposed to say.

'Good. Thank you,' I shrug modestly. I know my hair looks terrible. She's being kind. I run a hand over it again. 'How are you?'

'Er, yes, great, thank you.' She takes a breath and glances over to her friends. I see them watching us. I'm not like them. Not the typical "Mia friend," you might say. I'm not made from the same mould. 'OK, well, take care.'

I'm not sure what that actually means. Take care? Crossing the road? Using the iron? Driving the car?

I need to grab this opportunity. Seize upon it. It's my chance to capture this moment and turn it into a friendship. My heart suddenly lurches. This is it. This is the moment I've been waiting for. It takes me a moment to gather my thoughts and form some kind of non-lunatic sentence.

She beats me to it. 'Haven't I seen you in my spin class?' She smiles genuinely and I feel warmth radiate off her towards me. She knows she has. 'Yes, I think I have. Sorry I didn't recognise you. Your hair. It threw me for a moment.' She clearly hates my hair. I knew it was probably a mistake to have it done.

'Oh, sure. I've been a couple of times.' I stumble over my words. '*They* tell me it's supposed to be good for me.' I roll my eyes — again — as I say *they*. She won't know who *they* are, of course. I just sound bonkers to her. I can see it in her eyes.

'OK,' she says, and I can see she's trying to work out what I meant by *they*. 'That's good. Anyway. I need to get back. Nice to see you.' She heads off to her friends and I curse my missed opportunity. I think my new haircut might have scared her.

Mia has a girlie lunchtime get together once a month at her place, which, as I've mentioned, is close to mine. She serves up herbal teas, lattes made with a Gaggia espresso machine, wholesome cookies and homemade fruit bread. It's a drop-in session, which most of the village knows about. There are never fewer than eight people gathered in her countrified kitchen. It's always presided over by Ricky. He's never too far from Mia's side.

The kitchen is gorgeous, by the way, right out of a magazine. There's the pine kitchen table, squishy turquoise velvet sofa, comfy occasional chairs and two extremely well-behaved golden retrievers called Stan and Ollie. There are accented walls in turquoise with scatter cushions to match. I went once just to see inside her house, but I didn't stay long. I didn't want anyone asking me any questions. I merged into the background. I'm good at that. I dressed up for the occasion, even put on some make-up. I looked all over that house while I was there. Poked around. I even sneaked upstairs and tried on some of her perfume. Checked out her wardrobe and inside her drawers. Lay on her bed and spread my arms out on top of her silky grey bedspread. She has nice clothes and expensive perfumes and lotions. She owns a big house. Expensive. Tasteful. Pretentious. I didn't stay long. I got the feeling Ricky was a bit odd, though, always following her around. He gave me the creeps.

Today is my day off, which is why I'm sat here in this pub. Drinking expensive wine and stalking Mia. I am housekeeper at the Dahlia Hotel, a few miles from home. It's a sort of stopgap job. Not the best but it's fine for the moment. It's a low profile sort of job, kind of fits my needs if you know what I mean. It's not officially my day off. It's a sick day. I couldn't face going into work. I woke up this morning and thought, today is a crap day. It's raining. It's overcast. It's cold. I get masses of days like these, whatever the weather.

My boss, Jack Torres, wanted me there today to oversee the plumber. His English isn't brilliant, heavily accented and hard to understand, and he isn't good at dealing with sanitary problems. Like me? We are always getting blocked toilets, caused by idiots flushing nappies. What brain dead moron flushes a nappy down the toilet? Regardless, I wasn't in the mood. It's his hotel. Let him deal with it. He's been phoning but after my initial call this morning to tell him I was sick, I've ignored his calls.

Jack and I get on, for the most part. He's from Cuba. He looks like a drug lord, sports a bushy black moustache, heavily pockmarked face, black hair to his nape and very round at the waist. I imagine him falling over. He wouldn't be capable of righting himself, much like a turtle. I dislike him but then again, I dislike most people.

I studied Spanish in college, along with French. Foreign languages were my major. Jack needs me you see; sometimes he plays on his imperfect broken English to force me do more than my job description. On the odd occasion I don't mind, but he pushes his luck too often.

'Come on, Lindy, you and your husband can come and eat here for free if you do this for me.'

'Instead of paying me extra, you mean?'

Jack has a shrug all his own, it makes his neck disappear. 'Now, Lindy, you know I not think like this. How you like to come here for dinner? I put candles out, make the snug in the back of the restaurant special for you. What you think of that?'

'I think I want paying.'

'You Americans. All you think about is money.' He throws his hands up in despair.

'Because we can't live without it.'

13

Jack has produced five children. All of them look like mini Jacks, without the moustache. His wife looks harassed all the time. She never smiles. She has a hairstyle right out of the 1950s. I don't bother with her, she wears her pursed lips like a badge of honour. I can't imagine them having sex. At all. Ever. Clearly, they have at some point. The five uglies are proof of that. Frankly, I really can't be bothered with any of them. I just want to do my job and go home. I'm sounding bitchy. I can be. I have every right to be. Life sucks, and the cards it dealt me were the shittiest ever.

Jack's a little free with his hands at times. Standing too close to me when there's no need and "accidentally" touching my breasts. Then laughing and brushing his bushy, ugly, black moustache with his hand like Hercule Poirot.

'I could sue you for sexual harassment, you dirty perv.'

'Yes, you could, but you won't because you need this job,' he retorts in his thickly accented voice.

More's the pity.

Mia laughs at something one of the girls has said. I turn to watch them.

She doesn't mean to flirt; she just can't help herself. It's intrinsic, like breathing. She smiles at the bartender who has suddenly appeared at their table as if by magic.

Mia is a stunning woman. She has ash blonde hair cut into a bob with a heavy fringe. Thick, false eyelashes and skin so clear that even sweating in the spin class, she looks fabulous. I've had my hair cut in a similar style; not wanting her to think I was copying, I had it done a little different. There's no fringe and it's longer than hers. But still a bob. Whereas Mia's falls softly around her face and is beautifully cut, mine looks as if a blind person with a drink problem got hold of the scissors.

The bartender pulls out her chair and helps her get comfortable. Everyone else has to fend for themselves. Mia smiles at me from her seat. I realise I'm staring at her.

To Mia I'm one of those invisible people. She comes to the hotel with her husband, Ricky. Dicky Ricky is what I call him. He's out of his league and he adores her. Or so it seems. He is so full of himself. I don't fathom what she sees in him at all. I strongly suspect Dicky Ricky is not all he makes out to be.

Their marriage intrigues me. She's composed and elegant. He is smarmy and I don't quite trust him. I don't have any reason to feel that way. He strikes me as a gold digger. They have date nights. Ugh, date nights when you're married. Who in their right mind has date nights when they're married!

They always sit at the alcove table. That's where Jack wants Frank and I to sit for our never-going-to-happen free dinner. It's nice and private. Many couples request it when booking. On one occasion, I witnessed a guy put his hand under the table and bring his girlfriend off. I was shocked. Shocked they had the courage to do it in public and shocked that it turned me on. I think of Frank and choke on my wine.

When Mia and Ricky eat at the hotel — which is one of the reasons I got the job there — she's always gracious and charming to the staff. He says very little. Last time they were there, before the shopping bag incident at the supermarket, I made certain I was nearby when she visited the loo. He rarely leaves her side. We chatted over the hand basin. Like you do. I made polite conversation. Like you do. 'That's a lovely dress. You look stunning in it; it must be a special occasion,' I said. I think I was a little over the top and scared her. It was true though; it was a beautiful designer dress. And I *was* over the top.

She stiffened at first, and said nothing. Then she recognised my uniform and chilled out. I think she'd thought I was hitting on her. Maybe I was. Who knows what goes on in my messed-up head these days? I've never done it with a woman but if I did, Mia would be my choice. 'We have date nights,' she said, applying lipstick. It tinted her lips a luscious red colour. I imagined them all over Dicky Ricky's body. Over his cock. I bet they have dirty sex and a lot of it. 'We really like it here. It's not too far from home so Ricky can risk a drink or two.'

A drink driver, well, well. Another selfish twat. A flash of rage engulfs me. What a wanker. No surprise there, though. I picture him grabbing his keys after drinking several too many, thinking, *I'm Ricky Hicks what's the worst that can happen.* The hairs on the back of my neck stand up. I changed the subject, quickly. I was surprised to come out of the ladies with Mia and find Ricky waiting. She blushed. She turned from me, linked his arm and went back to their table, where they sat all loved up and cosied into each other.

So now I order some bar food, observing Mia in the mirror behind the whisky and the myriad bottles of gin. Such a popular drink these days. Frank and I used to drink gin in our day. We were big on gin. Bombay Sapphire was our tipple. A gin and tonic after work did just the trick. A few more then something to eat before returning home. The bartender is busy watching Mia. She answers her phone and looks annoyed. Probably Ricky telling her how much he worships her. She's probably heard it a million times. I guess it can get boring if someone keeps telling you. Moderation in everything.

We're both around a similar age. That's in our late forties. In your forties you still have the mindset of a thirty-year-old, only now you know how fucked-up the world is.

I'm nothing like Mia. The menopause has hit me hard. My hair is thinning. I'm putting on weight I can't shift. Not that I care. I've cut down so much on my food intake I'm miserably hungry. My clothes are too tight. So I don't bother. What's the point? What is the point of a lot of things actually? Another Ed Sheeran track comes on, I shake my head.

Mia exercises regularly. I don't. I get depressed and can't be bothered. I forget stuff unless it's scribbled down. I can be talking with someone, a customer, and lose the thread of the conversation just like that. Or I forget a common word. I go upstairs for something and forget what I went for. Go to the supermarket without a list? Disaster. I can't imagine Mia suffers with any of that. She doesn't look as if she does. I can take HRT. I'm told it might help. I don't want to. I don't see the point. You see, I don't want help. The doctor always asks too many of those questions I don't want to answer. So, I keep quiet, and that makes them think I'm depressed. 'Well, actually, Doctor, you might be right, but is it any surprise?' Idiot. They're all idiots. They think they can stitch up my mortal wound with a "It will all be better if you talk about it, Mrs Villas. Why not see a counsellor, Mrs Villas? Therapy is very helpful, Mrs Villas. Talking about it will help you come to terms with it, Mrs Villas." Fuck off, Doctor, Mrs Villas does not want to come to terms with it. Harsh, I know, but it's how I feel.

I call the bartender over. If I don't eat something, I'll pass out. 'Excuse me, Bartender?' He's been polishing the same glass since he got back to the bar. 'Bartender? Hello?' He's in a daze, eyes on Mia, and doesn't hear me call. I could go up in flames and he wouldn't notice. 'HEY!' I yell. That gets me noticed. 'I want my food; any time soon would be great.'

He strolls over to the kitchen. He couldn't care less whether my food is ready or not. His attention is focused on Mia one hundred percent. When he gets back to the bar, I can't help myself. 'Hey, love's young dream, she's out of your league and old enough to be your mother. Get a grip.' That shatters the young colt. His face drops in shock and surprise. What? Hasn't anyone spoken to him like that before? Christ, probably not. This younger generation are so delicate. Good grief.

'Do you want a *side* with your meal?'

I arch an eyebrow. Ooh, such malice. A side of what? His fist? 'No, thank you.' He disappears into the kitchen.

'Hi, thanks for that.'

I turn around. Mia is by my side, smiling. I'm embarrassed and shift in my seat. She wasn't meant to hear. 'Sorry, I'm ravenous, and the guy just isn't on the planet.'

'You're American, aren't you? Southern?'

I want to do my typical sigh. My accent, so unmistakable; how could anyone not notice? I'd have thought she'd have

17

cottoned on when we first met in the supermarket car park. This question annoys the hell out of me and usually prompts me to retort, "No, I'm English, I just watch lots of American movies." Or, "Really? I have an accent?" I don't say any of that to Mia.

'Yep. One hundred percent Yank. We're a bit forward and in your face. Guess you thought I was a bit blunt.'

'Not at all. I wish you were my bodyguard.' She blushes and looks away.

'You need a bodyguard? Why?'

She changes the subject. 'You work at that hotel, the Dahlia, don't you? I remember now. We spoke in the ladies. You liked my dress.'

Mia watches what she eats. She doesn't have desserts. Never eats chocolate. Always has skinny lattes made with almond milk. I'm highly allergic to cow's milk and also drink almond milk. That's another sign we're meant to be buddies. And she never goes out without makeup on. She gets her nails done at Heavenly Nails. She has massages at the beauty salon in Holmes Chapel, Gorgeous Beauty. Goes out every Monday with her girlfriends and Ricky picks her up, always. I'm sensing she's a little anxious right now. We carry on chatting and I get the distinct feeling she wants to ask me something only she hasn't the courage.

I think we are going to be the best of friends soon. I know, I sound creepy. So what? Maybe I am.

CHAPTER 2

Mia

Ricky has discovered some personal letters in the loft that I'd written before Sally was born. We were having a clear-out and I'd forgotten they were there. I didn't even know they still existed. Had I known I would have burned them. The problem is, Ricky is using them to blackmail me.

Granny left me a substantial lump of money in her will. She also told me I was never to tell Ricky or anyone else that she'd left it for me. I guess she never trusted Ricky. Now he's forcing me to put his name on the account. The lying piece of shit. I prefer not to think about it; it only brings it all back. The idea of reliving that day makes me feel sick to my boots, not to mention terrified.

The thing is, I know Ricky is having an affair. He doesn't know I know this. Because Ricky thinks I'm too stupid to work it or anything else out. To Ricky, I'm the stay-at-home wife enjoying the lifestyle he provides with a little part-time job. I wish I could tackle him about it. I can't check up on him because he monitors everything I do and I'm scared of rocking the boat and giving him a reason to carry out his threats.

We're well-known around here, if I start asking questions or going out without informing him first, I'm bound to be found out. And I don't want that. He can be really mean. I blink back the tears. I don't know how I've got to this place, or how I've turned into this weak woman.

Since I found out, I've been looking at every woman with suspicion. If they smile at me, I wonder why. If they shift their eyes when I walk past, I wonder if it's her. I look at the women all around me — in my spin class, in the pub — asking myself: Is that her? Or her? Or her? What sort of woman has he gone for? Somebody like me? Or the complete opposite? Younger? Older? The same age? She'll be well-off, if not rich. Ricky won't shag someone beneath what he perceives to be his lofty status. What woman has an affair with a married man in a close-knit village like ours? She might not even be from around here. She could be someone at work. I've started scrutinising him on the morning TV. Is he over-familiar with any of the women? Is he flirting more than he normally does?

Sally, our eldest, left home two years ago. She lives in Manchester, in one of those swanky modern apartments in the city centre with her boyfriend. She writes freelance for *Good Housekeeping* magazine. She spends two days a week in London and the rest of the time she can work from home. I'm glad she's close by, I'm close to both my girls. But not so close that I'd tell them what their father is up to. I don't know why I wouldn't. I try to remain composed — it's the one thing that really annoys him. The fact that I'm not begging for mercy. My pretty silk scarf covers the finger marks. They are starting to fade, but my throat still feels painful.

Annie, our youngest, left home last year. She's not as far away as Sally. She's renting a house with her friend in Northwich. She works as a dental nurse at a cosmetic dentist called Bright Smile.

Ricky comes home early. I hear the low purr of the engine pulling up on the drive. I pull my cardigan on, drawing the sleeve over my bandaged wrist. He doesn't like to be reminded of what he's done.

'HEY!' he bellows, climbing the stairs. I watch from the landing, preparing myself. 'I see you're dressed. I've got a stomach bug and I can't keep anything down. I thought I'd come home.' *Thought you'd keep an eye on me, you mean.*

I advise him in a matter of fact way to stay off food for forty-eight hours and just sip water. Try as I might, I'm unable to inject any warmth into my words. He complains bitterly of stomach cramps, so I send him to bed and tell him I'll bring up some water and dry toast. I'm not sure if I believe he's sick. He's up to something.

'You're not going to work, are you?' he moans.

'Yes. Why?' My phone vibrates in my pocket but I daren't look at it.

'I'm ill. I need somebody to bring me drinks. Keep me hydrated.'

'I'll fetch you what you need before I go. I can't abandon my classes so late in the day. It wouldn't be fair to the others.'

'But you can abandon me. Leave me here, alone, while I'm sick. I'm your husband. Who comes first, them or me?' Ricky tightens his lips and glares at me.

My heart starts hammering. I know he's up to something. My hand shakes a little as I hand him the glass of water. *Stop it. Stop it. Don't let him see he's getting to you.*

'I've been thinking, Mia. Perhaps you should hand in your notice and stop working. After all, we don't need the money, and the house is starting to get neglected.'

I stare defiantly at him. I wasn't expecting this. 'What? Give up my classes? Why? It doesn't affect you. Anyway, we have a cleaner, Ricky.'

'I don't like it,' he chides. 'It might be a good idea to hand in your resignation today while I'm off sick.' He changes into what he calls his "loungewear" and the rest of us call it trackie bottoms and comfy top. What an idiot. 'You can call it in. You'll get your exercise doing the housework. I've cancelled the cleaner anyway, didn't I tell you?' I don't answer. 'She won't be coming anymore. I didn't trust her anyway.'

'Ricky! No.'

'Oh, stop being so oversensitive. I don't want you to work. End of. You can give them a call now.'

'I'm not handing in my resignation over the phone,' I tell him heatedly. So much for keeping calm. This is what he wants, for me to fly off the handle, a good excuse to hurt me. Knowing full well I should stop — I continue. 'So, you've decided I'm not going to work. Just like that. Marion has been with us for years, there's nothing wrong with her. I can't give up my job. It's the only thing that's keeping me sane.'

'Don't you think your duty is at home? Stop trying to undermine me.' Undermine him? 'After all it's only spin classes, it's not a serious job, not like mine. You never worked when the girls were young. Besides, I don't like people knowing you work. It's demeaning, as if I can't provide for you. No, it's best if you resign today. You won't have the time now anyway. Not if you're looking after this house all by yourself.' My thoughts turn to my sister, Beth. She won't like this and she'll want to interrogate Ricky. 'Beth will pose a minor problem, being so liberated. She doesn't like me, she'll think I'm pressurising you. You'll have to convince her otherwise. I don't want her bad-mouthing me, Mia. Do you hear me? You know what she's like. You'll tell her it was your idea. Yes, that's the best way forward. That way she won't have a reason to say bad things about me.'

Is he thinking that imprisoning me in my own home is going to make me change my mind? I know that's what he's thinking. I'm not a fool. 'Beth won't believe I'll be content to sit around the house all day. What do you care what she thinks anyway? You can't stand her.' Beth has never liked nor trusted Ricky. She won't believe a word of this. She's convinced Ricky married me because of my money and my family's position. He's always dropping his father–in-law's name into conversations.

'You won't be sitting around, you'll be cleaning and putting together delicious meals for when I come home. Like a proper wife.' His words make me cringe. I'm trapped. 'I've always hated having Marion cook for us. You always used to do it.' I did when the girls were young but that was a long time ago. When I went back to work, our cleaner Marion suggested doing the cooking. There's nothing wrong with her food, she's a wonderful cook. I have my independence and I love my job. I won't give it up.

'What if I don't want to?' I take a step back, conscious of how handy he's been recently.

'Don't be silly, Mia.' He narrows his vindictive eyes at me. 'You need to respect me,' he says firmly, watching me slowly back away towards the bedroom door. 'While we're on this *sensitive* topic, you should stop going to your meet up at the pub on Mondays. We'll put a stop to that too for a while and see how you get on at home. You'll be tired minding the house all day. The last thing you'll want is to go out in the evening.'

My parched throat tightens convulsively. 'I'm going to the gym to do today's class.' I turn around to leave. *I'm not talking about this anymore. He's not imprisoning me in my home. I won't let this happen.*

'You're not going to continue with that pathetic job.'

'It's not a *pathetic* job.'

'It's not a proper job, is it? My job is a proper job. I get paid proper money, not like you. Your job won't cover even half the bills. Think you'd survive financially without me?' He laughs. 'Of course, you have mummy and daddy, don't you? They'll give you all you need. Is that it? You don't think you need me anymore? Is that why you want to work? To get away from me?'

'Oh, don't start,' I say evenly. 'You're just trying to piss me off so you can give yourself an excuse to hurt me.'

'No, Mia,' he says icily, getting out of bed and sitting on the edge. He looks at me malevolently then stands up, moves forward and grabs my wrist. I'm not quick enough and wince as he squeezes tighter, pressing on my old bruises. 'I don't think you're listening to me. Remember what I know. I can destroy you.' He jerks me towards him until I'm so close I can feel his breath on my face. My wrist throbs.

'I'm not making the call,' I say.

He twists my wrist again, bringing tears to my eyes. 'You will make the call. Where's your phone?' I pull my arm free and stumble backward.

'Ricky, this is absurd. I'm not letting people down. It's unprofessional. You're foolish if you think you can imprison me here.' I'm more than a little afraid of him. He's been cruel for a while but this new phase is different. This is nasty and calculating. I don't want to be in here with him. The way he's looking at me sets me on edge. I back away, slowly.

'Call them, Mia.' Ricky shakes his head as if I'm some stupid kid. 'Clearly, I have to be firmer with you, because you're not getting the message, are you? It's not difficult, is it? If you put my name on the bank account, then all this can be rectified. Is there a reason why you don't trust me . . . darling?'

'You're not being fair, Ricky. It's not our money.'

'What do you imagine I'm going to do? You know I love you and the girls very much. I merely want to make things go smoothly in the tragic event of something terrible happening to you.'

Now I narrow my own eyes. 'Like what? There's nothing wrong with me.'

'Now. But who knows what the future might bring. Why make all our lives difficult? Let's say you were in an accident and were unconscious and on life support. Or you disappeared, maybe you fell off a boat or went hiking and got lost and nobody could find you. We'd be unable to access your bank account or any of your private papers. We'd have to wait seven years until you were legally deemed to be dead. Think of all the problems that would cause for your family. If you loved me, if you loved *us*, you wouldn't put us through that.'

'I do love the girls. I mean, I love my family. I understand what you're saying, but, Ricky, I don't go sailing or hiking. This isn't going to work.'

'Why don't we go away? Just the two of us. What do you say? It'll be fun spending time together. We could go on a sailing holiday around the Greek islands.'

My heart plummets. He's trying to force my hand. He wouldn't go as far as arranging an accident. Would he? The risks are too high. He isn't a risk-taker. Ricky enjoys an uncomplicated life. 'I'm not leaving my job and we're not going on holiday.'

Ricky smiles knowingly. 'You seem a little on edge, darling. Oh! How crass of me. Here I am talking about falling overboard and getting lost at sea, and then suggesting a sailing holiday. I wasn't thinking. I hope you haven't read anything into it. Mia, let me have your phone, please.' His arm snakes out and he pulls my phone from my pocket. 'Best you don't have this for a while. It'll make your transition to home a lot easier if you don't have contact with your friends. Actually, the more I think of it, it's best if you stay in the house for the next few weeks. I'll fetch you anything you need. It's difficult to make change work. I'll cancel your monthly coffee morning. Leave it to me, it'll be less embarrassing if I do it. No navigating all those tricky questions.'

I stand at the door, wondering what to do, and hear male voices downstairs. He can't keep me locked in here. He has my phone, but there's still the landline. I'll call my sister and ask her to come over. I am really worried now. I turn and leave the room, curious about what's going on downstairs, slipping through the door without another word.

Downstairs, I see workmen coming in and out of our front door. 'What are you doing here?' I ask one of them. How the hell did they get in?

'Your husband gave us a key. We're fitting new locks to the doors and windows. You must have forgotten we were coming. Happens to the best of us. Cup of tea would do nicely, if you don't mind?'

Ricky appears behind me. 'I thought you were ill,' I say.

'I'm better now.' He stretches out his hand and the man drops a set of keys in his palm. 'Thank you.'

'All the doors are done now and the downstairs windows. We'll get on upstairs if that's OK, then we'll be out of your way,' the joiner says, picking up his tools and heading for the stairs. 'Two sugars for me, none for Stu. Thanking you.'

'Ricky, what's going on?'

'There have been a lot of burglaries around here lately, so I thought we needed to improve security. I'm feeling much better by the way, and I'm hungry. Shouldn't you be in the kitchen preparing my lunch? Oh, and, Mia, don't forget their tea. They always do a better job if you ply them with tea and biscuits.'

'Make it yourself,' I say, going to open the front door. It's locked. 'Open the door, Ricky, and give me the keys, I'll make another set while I'm out.'

He pockets the keys. 'You won't be needing them. Now, go and make me some lunch. Or do you want me to call Sally?' We stare at each other. I'm trying to gauge if he really would call Sally and tell her what he discovered in my letters. I can't take the chance.

I make up a quick lunch for Ricky, aware of the camera spying on me. Ricky will be watching me on his phone app. We have a smart home that he manages by apps on his phone. We have cameras outside and in. We have cameras at the door, so we know who's calling. Inside, the app controls the lights. As well as the heating. We just ask Alexa. Our house has every gadget going. I long for an old-fashioned house, where you switch things on, plug things in. I put out two mugs, make the tea and take them to the joiners. I don't bother with biscuits.

The landline sits, impassive, on the windowsill. I should call Beth. And say what? My husband has turned into a psychopath, and in order to get his grasping hands on my money, he's locked me in my house?

I could call Sally to come over when Ricky is at work and tell her myself. I've no idea what her number is. It's in my contacts, in my phone. I don't know anyone's number off by heart apart from Beth's. I used to know the girls', but they've recently changed them. I could ring *Good Housekeeping* in London, explain and persuade them to give me her number.

They won't hand it out. They'll say they'll call her and ask her to phone me. Which is useless. I know, I'll write a letter! Good old-fashioned correspondence. I'll write to her, telling her I need to see her to discuss something delicate and not to speak to her dad about it. She's extremely devoted to him. She'll just call him and ask why I'm writing to her.

I set his food on the table, my hands shaking. How far is he going to go with this?

Ricky's job is in television. He's the anchor on a local breakfast show. He works in Media City in Manchester and loves his job. Everybody loves Ricky. Everyone should love Ricky because he's on the telly. He has over a million followers on Twitter. He never interacts with them; only posts pictures of himself doing this or that.

'Are you quite well, Mia? You seem anxious.' I jump. Suddenly he's at the kitchen door. 'Did you enjoy your time in the kitchen? You looked deep in thought. I hope you're not planning on doing anything to upset me. You know all I have to do is call Sally and tell her she's a bastard and her great-uncle is her father. Gosh, how that can of worms will destroy you all. I can see it now. I'll tell her I only just found out. Then I'll tell her she isn't any daughter of mine and that I'll have to disown her. She'll be pretty shattered, don't you think?'

I stare at him. 'Why? Why would you be so unspeakably cruel? It would be hurtful enough if she found out she wasn't yours, but to say those cruel things to her—'

'Will you *please* not tell me what I should say to my daughter!' he retorts.

'So you still regard her as your daughter then!'

'Enough!' he shouts, while upstairs, the builders are briefly quiet.

'You love her. Why would you want to hurt your daughter?'

He laughs humourlessly. 'That's the whole point, isn't it, Mia? She isn't my daughter.'

'You're her father. You brought her up. You can't disown her now! What sort of monster are you?'

'I guess you're discovering that now. But, Mia, I keep telling you. This doesn't need to happen if only you'd see sense and put my name on the accounts.'

Tears stream down my cheeks. I stifle a howl of pent-up rage that he's got me in this trap. It's only money. I appreciate that. But it's not my money, is it? It's my children's money, bequeathed to them by my beloved grandmother. It's not his to fritter away with his fancy woman. It's not *only* money.

I tell him he's fucked up. He doesn't appreciate that. He slaps me and throws me to the floor with a few well-placed punches that land where nobody will see. With an 'I'll see you later,' he walks over to the fridge and empties everything out into a couple of bin bags. 'Oh and by the way, I'm rationing your food. I did the pantry and the cupboards this morning, before you got up. I thought it best, I knew you'd make a scene. Soon, Mia, you will give me what I want.'

In the beginning Ricky was wonderful. Loving. Adoring. Everything a girl desires in a boyfriend. He charmed my parents and all my friends. He still does. The ideal husband to the outside world. At work they worship him. His fans adore him. The neighbours can't get enough of him. He is "Mister Popular" with a capital P. When he started this affair, he changed. He became nasty. Sarcastic. He never used to hit me.

I met Ricky at the Tatton Flower Show. He was there for work, representing a small TV network. Hungry for fame, he climbed the ladder of success, fast and ruthlessly. No one else stood a chance against his charm and good looks. Ricky can play to the audience like a well-trained actor. If he were an actor, he'd have shelves full of awards. His performances were magnificent: Caring Husband. Doting father. Loving son. Twat with a capital T.

I was with my parents that day. Ricky appeared by my side, saying, 'You'd look good on my arm, beautiful.' I didn't know how to respond. I knew it was a line — tacky and egotistical. I was also flattered.

He started up an animated conversation with my dad about gardening. It was one of those rare blisteringly hot weeks of unbroken sunshine we get in the UK from time to time. It was a beautiful day. Our trip to Tatton was a last-minute decision. I drove us there in my new soft-top convertible.

They were smitten with him. He was immediately invited for tea and to see dad's splendid gardens. We lived in Plumley in an elegant Victorian gentleman's villa. I had a privileged life. My parents were, and still are, loving and devoted to me. Except Ricky has them under his spell.

Dating Ricky had been a marvellous experience in the beginning. I fell deeply in love with this man who couldn't do enough for me. On our first date we went to Edinburgh and stayed at a magnificent hotel close to the castle. He was attentive, protective and gentle. He told me all about the wondrous places he'd been and about the funny things that had happened on set. I fell like a stone. I loved him so much I would have done anything for him.

We got engaged that weekend and were married within the year.

When I'm out with my friends and they chatter about their husbands and their marriages, I keep quiet. Ricky doesn't want me to discuss our private life. I have to reveal the odd thing, though, because it would look weird if all I said is how wonderful he is. I don't say much, trivial stuff mostly.

I can't believe he's taken all the food out of the house. I slam the cupboard door shut then open it again as if that will make the provisions magically reappear. No. It's still empty. Whoever this woman is, she really has got her claws into him.

CHAPTER 3

Lindy

I'm having to stay late because the pot wash hasn't turned up. Preparing a "round robin" text to find a stand-in, I fire it off to the staff. If we can't get anyone, Jack's told me I will have to stand in. I don't think so. I am not employed to wash dishes and he's got enough kids who can jump in and help. Mercifully, a text comes in from Samuel saying he'll do it.

Jumping into my ten-year-old Fiesta just after 6 p.m., I pull my shabby coat around me for warmth. The heating doesn't work and when it gets really cold the windows fog up and I have to drive with them down.

Driving towards our estate, I pass Mia's house and see that all the lights are on. The days are so short now. The temperature's dropped considerably since lunchtime. I've got goosebumps all over my skin and I'm shivering.

Dicky Ricky's BMW 6 series sits proudly in their gravelled drive next to Mia's BMW 4X4. Reversing into the drive of the vacant house opposite, I turn off the engine. I snuggle deep into my coat. It's not the best but it'll do for half an hour or so.

I've been coming here for a while. It's an excellent place to observe them from. To be honest, I'm surprised nobody has knocked on the window demanding to know what the hell I'm doing here.

Mia's is one of the more imposing houses on this exclusive estate. They don't close the curtains. I often wonder why. In the bedroom, Mia stands wrapped in a towel, she's turned to face someone coming into the room. Shuddering at the thought of having only a towel around me, I pull out my small binoculars from the glove compartment and zoom in. My hands are stiff from the cold.

They have a huge, low hanging chandelier over the bed. I wonder if they do it with the lights on or off? She's shivering, I can see her shaking. Surely it isn't cold in there? She needs to turn up the heating or put some warm clothes on, she'll catch a cold. Ricky appears, naked, with a towel in his hand. He is talking to her and rubbing her shoulders. I wish I could hear what they are saying. Maybe I could place some sort of microphone in the house on one of Mia's coffee mornings. It wouldn't be difficult. I know my way around their house. I've explored it, thoroughly. Too thoroughly? Perhaps.

He strokes her glossy hair. They look so in love standing there together. I bet he's telling her how beautiful she is. Oh my God, she's dropped her towel. Aah, she's teasing him. He's looking her over. I've seen things happen at this house that I'm betting nobody else knows. The sex they have! He likes to take her up against the wall, bent over the sofa.

Frank never ogles me like that, not now. Not that I'd give him the opportunity. I don't remember the last time he saw me naked. He used to look at me the way Ricky's looking at Mia. He used to tell me I had a gorgeous body. He used to take photos of me. I never look at them. That was another Lindy, a Lindy from long ago. Before my life changed.

A woman wrapped up in a huge grey puffa coat walks past with her bulldog. I smile to myself. They say dog owners take after their dogs. She doesn't glance my way. I drop my binoculars and slide down in my seat. The dog defecates on Mia's front lawn. The woman takes a small black bag and picks it up. They continue on their way.

I know everything about Mia. I know when Ricky goes to work and what time she leaves for the gym and the times she pops back during the day. She likes a Costa coffee at about eleven. She takes a shower before Ricky gets home. I've seen her in Waitrose. Unlike me, she can afford to shop there. She buys organic, she can afford that too. Although, sometimes, I do see her buying those cheese slices kids like in their sandwiches. She buys Galaxy chocolate. And chocolate-coated peanuts. I reckon she's a secret nibbler.

I watched Ricky on TV this morning. He's so attractive. So full of life and cheer. Ricky always looks sleek and contented. You can tell he loves his job. Why not, it's a brilliant job. Who wouldn't like it? They have the perfect marriage. They're loved in the community. They do a lot for charity. They are perfect. So perfect they're not quite real. Can anything be that bloody perfect?

Frank doesn't work. Not anymore. He did. But not now. Now he does nothing. Nothing at all. He stays in the house all day, doesn't go out. Doesn't help. Won't help himself. Frank used to be handsome. Not as handsome as Ricky, but he was tall and slender with beautiful hands. I loved his hands, his long slender fingers. I used to like watching them glide over my body. He always wore a moustache. As a rule, I dislike facial hair but I liked Frank's moustache. He bites his nails now. His hands are ugly. He's put on weight. He has high cholesterol. His hair is too long and he needs to do something about his nasal hair. You're probably thinking I should help him. But you don't know the whole story.

When we first met, we were flying high. Ambitious. We met at the firm of architects where we were both employed. Back in the States I majored in languages at college. But when I came to the UK, I did a fast-track course in architecture. The company occupied a charming office off Spring Gardens in

Manchester city centre, the very latest in post-modern building design. We used to lunch together every day and grab a drink after work before heading home. There were always parties and we went to most of them. We were respected professionals in the world of architecture, winning most of the commissions we pitched for. We were known as the golden couple. We opened our own company — LF Architects. Business was good, we employed twenty-five people and we prospered. After we married and had the kids, I went back to work part-time. We were living the dream. How many times did we congratulate each other. We told ourselves we were blessed. We thought we were untouchable. Launched on a never-ending roll. But all rolls have to come to an end sometime, don't they? Ours did. With a crunch.

Mia's children come to visit about once a month. She has two girls, Annie and Sally. They look alike, they look like Mia with Ricky's height. I don't know where they live but it can't be far away, they come too often. They sit in the dining room enjoying a meal cooked by Mia. With my binoculars I can see them clearly, laughing, eating, behaving like a normal family should. I think it's mostly a roast dinner. I can see it being served. It looks delicious and I want to join them. I picture myself striding up to the front door and saying, 'Hey there, that looks great, mind if I join you?' I snigger. I can just picture their faces.

The other night at the pub where love's young dream drooled over Mia, a guy tried to pick me up. I know, you're surprised, but you couldn't be more surprised than me. It's true I had made an effort that evening, for a change. Not much of one I admit, but it was an effort nonetheless. Mia wouldn't have spoken to me if I looked like I do right now. I sniff the lapel of my coat and wrinkle my nose. I think it was probably the first time in forever that such a thing happened. The guy was overweight but nicely dressed in a tailored suit. He looked sharp — a bit like Frank used to. Nice hands. Good haircut and clearly well off. I saw him pay with big notes. Why the hell he wanted to chat me up still baffles me. I was blunt and rude and generally unpleasant, but he was persistent in that semi-aggressive manner guys have when they're not getting their own way. He kept his eyes on my breasts. Are you surprised? I guess I forgot to tell you I have a "good rack" as they say in the States.

It did enter my mind to shepherd him round to the back of the pub and fuck him. I could have said, 'Hey, buddy, I can see you've got a stiff one. Wanna go around the back and fuck?' Men like it when you talk dirty. Weird, aren't they? He'd say, 'Only if you touch me now, then give me a blow job.' I'd reach inside his pants and watch his face contort. We'd go outside, I'd pull off my knickers and straddle him, up against the cold brick wall with the acrid kitchen smells drifting around us as he puffed and grinded me into the brickwork. He'd come. I wouldn't. Sometimes I get a mad urge to do reckless things. Not that night.

CHAPTER 4

Mia

I'm turning forty-five today and we've booked a table at the Dahlia. My parents are coming and the girls with their partners. Plus my two sisters, Beth and Zoe. We're staying over at the hotel so we don't have to worry about getting home. It was Ricky's idea. We're paying for everything. My parents tried to insist, but Ricky can be stubborn like that.

It's the first time I've been allowed out of the house in days, and the thought of food has been driving me slowly mad all day. I can't stop salivating. I've drunk so much water to keep my hunger at bay that I'm bloated. I searched the house and found some rancid peanuts in a coat pocket. I ate them. What was I going to do? Throw them away? Not likely. This is the first time he's given me no food at all.

I'm driving the girls to the hotel. Ricky told me this morning so I've had time to prepare what I'm going to say. How I should act. I'm surprised he told the girls to come to the house. I decided I would snatch a moment to speak to Sally privately and tell her. That's what I'd planned, but when the moment arose, I couldn't find the words. They choked me. I pictured her beautiful face crumbling. Her whole life collapsing in front of me. Ricky knew I wouldn't be able to do it. Anyway, I was aware of him listening to my every word, watching my every move.

Now we stand in the hallway, the three of us ready to go. A slight awkwardness has suddenly arisen between us. The girls have noticed I'm not myself. They haven't said anything and I've forestalled the uncomfortable questions. I've lost weight and they're concerned about me. 'I had a stomach bug for a few days but I'm OK now,' I say chirpily.

'Should you be going out so soon then?' Sally asks.

'Oh, yes, it was only a couple of days. You know how quickly I lose weight if I don't eat,' I say. They don't, but it's all I can think of. As if I'm going to miss out on this meal. I'm chomping at the bit, desperate to get there and stuff my face. I've spent the day trying to take my mind off food. It's been impossible. The TV is full of food adverts, the radio too. I had to switch them off before they drove me insane.

'Mum? It's not something serious you're not telling us about, is it?' Sally asks, topping up her lipstick in the hall mirror.

I don't understand what she means. Do they know? Then I realise she's asking if I have cancer and I'm keeping it from them. 'No, no. It's like I said, a stomach bug.' I button up my coat, check I have the house key Ricky let me have for tonight, and pull open the door. Perhaps I can pretend to lose the key so I can get a copy made. He'd only change the locks again.

Earlier in the day Ricky came home and, eating a chocolate bar in front of me, told me what a mess I looked. 'You'd better sort yourself out, Mia. I won't have your family thinking I'm neglecting you. And don't even consider speaking to them about what is happening at home. Otherwise I will tell them your secret.' He pulled out the letter from his jacket pocket and waved it in front of me. 'I'll have this with me just in case you decide to call my bluff.'

Ricky will be joining us a little later. He said he had a couple of meetings late in the day and wanted to miss the rush hour traffic. He dropped the chocolate wrapper in the kitchen bin. After he left, I took it out and licked it. I hate what he is making me do.

We're eating early, at seven. My parents like to have early nights, lights out by 10 p.m. Fine by me; the earlier the better. I want to get some time alone with Beth, even if it's just five minutes. I need to tell her about Ricky. I need her to help me.

I drive out of our estate and pick up the A34 for the short journey to the hotel. I'm light-headed from lack of food and have to force myself to concentrate on the road. It doesn't help that it's dark and there aren't many street lights.

'Are you OK, Mum? You're driving really slow. It's annoying the drivers behind.'

I glance in the rearview mirror and see the queue building. I'm on edge, afraid my family will sense something is wrong and start interrogating me in front of Ricky. I put my foot down a little more, the car jerks as I miss the gear. I clutch the steering wheel in both hands like a new driver. My mind is all over the place with worry. Will Mum notice something isn't right between us? Beth will, I'm sure. We're close; she always picks up when I'm having an off day. Growing up it was always the two of us against Zoe. Zoe was always a little off, not quite mainstream. It drove Mum and Dad potty. Why does she always have to be *different*, Mum would say.

I'm unable to concentrate on the road for long. My thoughts turn towards my family and the pain it will cause them if they find out my secret. I veer over the white line. An oncoming car swerves and sounds its horn. 'Mum!' shouts Sally. I swing back into my lane. I'm scared to speak out about Ricky but I have to tell Beth. She's the only one I can tell. She'll know what to do. Beth is practical.

'Sorry.' I glance at her with a meek smile and look back at the road.

I've been a fool to allow it to get this bad. My stomach is making sounds like a blocked drain. Next to me, Sally looks in my direction.

I force a laugh. 'Stop looking at me like that. Honestly, I'm simply hungry, that's all. I've not had time to eat much today.'

Will I even be able to eat politely? I have a vision of myself piling fistfuls of food into my mouth, while they look on, horrified. I tell myself to come back to planet normal. It can't happen. I have to control myself.

'Here. Turn here, Mum,' shouts Annie from the backseat. I swerve off the main road without indicating, and onto the narrow country lane, mounting the verge as I turn in towards the hotel.

The Dahlia Hotel is a Grade II listed building situated next to St Ives Church just a mile from the A34. It dates from the early nineteenth century. The front is white brick with a central Doric porch. The two storey five sash-window bays are set in an arcade with a pair of dormers, also with sashes. The three centre bays have a pediment. There is an overhanging hipped roof with wooden bracketed eaves, and in the garden a magnificent giant redwood tree adds to the splendour of the place. It was a private school for a long time, then fell into disrepair until Jack Torres acquired it.

Ricky completely threw me when he said he'd be delayed. What did he mean by it? Surely, he'd have wanted to be with me in case I said something to my family? Mum thinks he's delightfully eccentric. She won't hear a bad word about him. 'You're so lucky to have found a man like Ricky, Mia. He's wonderful. So thoughtful. He sent me some flowers the other day. The card read *"just because you're my mother-in-law."*' She's besotted with him. I don't think I'll find an ally there.

Today he came home with a new handbag. He said I should get my hair done differently. 'You're looking staid, showing your age.'

'But there's no chance I'll get an appointment now, Ricky. You know how busy Thomas is.' It struck me that if I'd been smarter, I could have gone to the hairdressers and asked them for help.

'You'd better make yourself look good. You know what your sisters are like. Always quick to criticise me. Especially Beth.'

'That's not true; they love you.' They won't once they find out what he's doing to me. I'll think of a way to get to speak to Beth tonight. It'll be difficult. He's too clever not to spot it. All the things that can possibly go wrong rush into my mind. He'll bully me. He'll hit me later, that's a certainty. But I won't let go of that money granny left me. I must keep control of that little part of me that is mine. Just in case. I will find a solution. A way out. He's not going to win. He won't let me starve to death. What use would that be to him? No, clever Ricky is feeding me just enough to keep me alive, while making me suffer both physically and psychologically.

I stand in the foyer of the hotel holding my new Mulberry handbag. The aroma coming from the kitchen hits me as soon as I walk in, making me giddy with longing. My stomach lets out an almighty gurgle. Saliva pools in my mouth, threatening to run down my chin.

Sally and Annie remove their coats and hand them to the porter. I do the same.

Mum and Dad are already seated. I can see them through the glass doors leading into the restaurant. It's busy in here tonight. I nod to a couple of people I know, but daren't go over in case Ricky disapproves and makes me pay for it later.

They have the fire lit. The room looks cosy, welcoming. We've been seated close to the open fire. I stumble and almost fall when I see Ricky already there with my parents. I hadn't noticed him at first, he must have been hidden from view by one of the waiters. Sally catches me. 'You sure you're OK, Mum?' I might have known he'd never leave me free to snatch a moment with Beth.

'Yes, I'm fine, darling, thank you.' I take her arm and the three of us walk towards the table.

Mum waves happily, beckoning me over. At the table I make for the chair next to Beth, but digging his fingers into my painful wrist, Ricky quickly pulls me to his side.

'I thought you were going to be late,' I say, nervously. Any confidence I may have had is gone. He's done this to unsettle me. Well, it worked.

'Darling, you look gorgeous,' Mum says. 'Ricky, let her sit next to Beth, they haven't chatted in ages. You can't monopolise her all the time.' She pats the chair beside Beth. I start to get up again. He can't possibly object now Mum has asked me, but he tightens his hold and I stay put.

'I haven't seen Mia all day and I did want to speak to her about something. Perhaps she can move over there later, when they're serving dessert. Annie, go on, sit next to your auntie.' He leans into me and whispers, 'I wanted to surprise you, sweetie. It is your birthday. I knew you'd try to speak with Beth and you didn't disappoint me. Headed right for her, didn't you? Silly bitch.'

I see Beth's face fall but only for a second. She sends Ricky a broad smile, then begins chatting to Annie and Sally while their partners sit beside them looking bored.

Ricky smiles back. 'Feel free to tell Beth about how terrible your husband is to you,' he suggests. 'See how far that gets you.' He turns to the table. 'Mia wants to tell Beth something. Go on, darling. What did you want to say?'

I shrink into my seat and shake my head. 'Nothing. It was nothing. Ricky's being silly.' What a bastard. I yank my wrist out of his grip and shunt my chair away from him as far as I dare.

We order our drinks. Beth stands up and comes to my side, to offer a toast to my birthday. She places two silver balloons weighted down by silver hearts in front of me. 'Here you are, Mia, old thing. Hope you like your prezzy.' Wrapping her arm around my shoulders, she pulls me into her, tight. Kisses me on the cheek and whispers, 'I know something is wrong. I've been trying to call you.' Then she pulls away and announces, 'I didn't know what to get you, so I got you something practical.' Beth and Zoe clap, and everyone sings *Happy Birthday*. I put on a smile and do my best to pretend I'm having a great time, while all I can think of is the delicious meal that's coming. And how soon I can escape the watching eyes of my family so I can go home and cry.

I gulp. 'Can't wait. I'll open them at home if that's OK with everyone.' I feel my eyes well up. I want desperately to tell them what's going on. Beth rubs my back soothingly. It only makes me feel worse.

'Mia!' Mum says, oblivious. How can she be so blind to what he's doing? 'Open them now, darling. Come on, it's your birthday. We all want to see what you got. Ricky, what did you get her? Something fabulous as usual, I'm sure.' She raises her glass.

'Of course,' he says smugly, making me cringe. 'Only the best for my fabulous wife.' He kisses me on the cheek and strokes my hand. Instinctively, I almost pull it away. I don't. Sally and Annie are all smiles. His thumb presses into the underside of my wrist. My other hand, resting on the table next to my cutlery, clenches reflexively into a fist. Beth notices and I relax it.

'So, Ricky, what did you get Mia?' Beth asks, staring him down. His grip on my wrist tightens. I try to pull my hand away but he tightens his grip. He's hurting me so much it's hard to stop myself crying out.

'Show them, darling. Mia wanted a new handbag. Didn't you, darling? Is this it, sweetheart?' He takes my new Mulberry from me and places it on the table. 'I know she has a lot of them, but I can't deny her anything. Isn't that right, Mia? I spoil you too much, don't I?'

Listen to him. Mr Wonderful. Mum gushes about how lucky I am to have found such a wonderful man. I experience a sudden urge to stick my fork into his face.

'Yes, Ricky *spoils* me all the time.' I smile, too brightly, unable to make eye contact with any of them. Instead, I focus my gaze just over the tops of their heads.

He gives everyone his Colgate smile. Beth's present is forgotten, just as Ricky intended.

Beth is looking over. She's looking at Ricky's grip on my wrist. I place my other hand over it.

Beth is the only one of them who hasn't fallen for Ricky's charm. I have a feeling she actually detests him. Whenever they meet they end up fighting about something, and then he takes it out on me when we're alone.

'Mia?' she says now. 'Have you had your nails done? Let me see. Oh, I love that colour.' She pulls my hand towards her, forcing Ricky to let go. I had them done ages ago, before all this started. Now they've grown out and the varnish has begun to peel off. I see his jaw tighten. Beth takes my hands in hers. 'You always did have perfectly shaped nails. They need re-doing, though. When are you going back?' She turns my hands over, looking at my bruised wrists. 'We should go together.'

I pull away. 'Oh. Sometime soon. I need to make an appointment. I'm starving. Can we order?' I purloin a bread roll from the bread basket in the centre of the table. I tear a chunk off and devour it, aware of his eyes on me. I try not to stuff myself, although it's hard to resist. I catch sight of the butter. When did I last have butter? I coat the bread with it, biting down, ripping another chunk off with my teeth. I'm aware of nothing but the sheer pleasure of eating. I never realised how good bread tastes.

Annie and Sally catch up with my parents. Their partners engage Ricky in eager conversation. Which famous people has he met and which celebrity parties has he attended. Ricky responds, turning the force of his charm on them but I know he's listening to every word I say.

'Ricky?' Beth asks. 'You won't mind if Mia and I go off for a spa day, will you? It's part of my birthday present to her. Won't that be wonderful, Mia, a whole day of being pampered!'

Ricky's thigh presses against mine.

'Yes, it would, Beth,' I say brightly. The pressure against my thigh increases. 'But spas aren't really my thing,' I say, wanting to cry. Beth gives me a look as if to say, *What the hell are you talking about? You love spas.*

'Nonsense, darling, you must go. Why don't you set it up, Beth, and let us know the dates? I'll pencil it in the diary so we don't forget. We have so much on at the moment, don't we, darling?'

I know what he's playing at. All willing to indulge his lovely wife, but when we get home, he'll say, 'You agree to the date and pull out the night before.'

Before I know it, the waiters are clearing our main courses and have brought the dessert menus. I've eaten too much and because I haven't eaten properly in days, my stomach is protesting. I want more but I'll throw up if I do. I want to lie down. I need to let all the glorious food digest. I shift uncomfortably in my chair.

I catch sight of Lindy. What's she doing here? Of course, she works here. She smiles and I smile back. Ricky notices. 'Who's that?'

'Lindy. She works here and goes to my spin class.'

'She doesn't look like your type of friend.'

'What is my type of friend, Ricky?' I retort, only to be pinched on the thigh for my cheek.

'Don't get stroppy with me,' he hisses in my ear. 'I don't like the look of her. Ignore her.' I see Beth watching.

'Why? Because she has a job? Looks normal? *Likes* me?'

'Precisely.'

'That's settled then, Mia,' Beth announces. 'I'll look into it tomorrow and give you a call. Zoe, I'd ask you but I know spas are definitely not your thing.'

Zoe is your typical earth mother. She lives in an organic house, decorated with organic paint. She only eats vegetables from her organic garden. She even had a falling out with her neighbour because they used weedkiller. Apparently, it was running under the fence into her garden. She's fallen out with most of her neighbours now, over one thing and another.

She wasn't always like that, but five years ago she went to India for a cleansing. When she returned, she divorced Simon. She had become so far removed from the Zoe we all knew that we reckoned she must have been brainwashed.

'No they're not, Beth. But there's no need to be so snidey about it. Just because you can't accept my beliefs it doesn't give you the right to attack me.'

'Oh, shut up, will you. You're so sensitive these days you're like a bloody teenager,' Beth says.

'Let's not fall out tonight, please.' Dad is standing up to make a toast. He clinks his glass with the edge of a fork. 'I want to wish you a marvellous birthday, Mia. You were our last born and we worried about you. You were never as plucky or confident as your sisters. So when you met Ricky, we couldn't have been happier for you. Let's all raise a glass to Mia.'

Ricky squeezes my thigh and whispers, 'Say something nice, darling. Tell them how happy you are.'

I raise my glass. 'Thanks, Dad. This has been wonderful, having you all here tonight. It's not often we get together like this. I am very lucky to have found Ricky. Why don't you all come over to the house next week? I'll cook.' Ricky pinches me hard on the leg and I let out a squeal.

'Come on, Mia, spill the beans on dear Ricky. Hasn't he got any faults?'

'Auntie Beth, how can you say such a thing about Dad!'

'I'm only kidding, Sally.'

'Put a sock in it, Beth. You've had too much to drink — again. You always get bitchy when you drink. So she loves her husband and doesn't want to talk about all the little niggly things. Why should she?' Zoe says.

'Girls,' Mum says. 'That's enough. This is Mia's birthday, don't ruin it. We all appreciate you've been unlucky in that department, Beth, but there's no need to be bitter. Mia, we'd love to come over. Just tell us when.'

'Come on, Mum. That's unfair,' says Beth. 'It was hardly my fault that Tony decided he's gay.'

'I'm not discussing it here. Who's having dessert?'

'Mia, have something, please,' Beth says. 'Share one with me if you don't want a whole one. Come on, you look like you need fattening up. Whatever this diet is that you're on, it's obviously not doing you any good. You don't look well.'

'Oh, really, Beth, I'm pretty stuffed. Maybe share one with the girls.'

'Go on, darling, spoil yourself. It is your birthday after all.' Ricky picks up the dessert menu. 'What do you fancy, Beth? The chocolate mousse? Mia loves chocolate mousse.' With Ricky staring at me I have no choice but to acquiesce. 'By the way, I think Mia has forgotten what a hectic week we have. In fact, we are busy for the next few weeks, plus I have a lot of things going on at work. I'm afraid we'll have to postpone that dinner. We'll be in touch. Won't we, Mia? Your memory is getting worse, you know.'

I look at Ricky. He's forcing me to eat dessert, knowing I'll probably be sick. 'Yes, I forgot,' I say. 'We are busy, aren't we? Sorry, Mum.'

'Oh, never mind. Let us know when you're free.' She looks disappointed. I've let her down, and I want to rush over to her and tell her Ricky is not the man she thinks he is. Tell her he beats me, starves me, and now is blackmailing me, threatening to destroy our family. She wouldn't hear of it. Darling Ricky? Never! She'd likely tell me I was undergoing some mid-life crisis. I'd obviously fallen out with him over something but demonising him to her family was not the way to put it right.

'Oh, by the way,' Beth interrupts, ignoring Ricky. 'What are you doing tomorrow?'

'Why don't you share the mousse with Beth?' Ricky says.

I blink. Which question to answer first? It's probably politic to answer Ricky. 'I'll pass on the mousse. I really am too full.'

I see the rage gathering in his eyes. 'No. I'd like you to have it. It's your birthday.' He pushes his thigh firmly against mine.

'OK, Beth.' My voice falters. 'Let's . . . order the chocolate mousse.'

The waiter comes over to take our order. He stands next to Mum, smiling across at Sally, who coyly smiles back from beneath her eyelashes and gets a shove from her boyfriend for it. She catches me watching and blushes.

'Mum, order us a chocolate mousse will you?' Beth says. 'Mia and I are sharing. So. Are you busy tomorrow, Mia? Aren't you going to some do at Media City, Ricky?'

He takes in a deep breath, clearly annoyed that she's persisting with the question. My heart beats wildly. What's she planning? She shouldn't have said she knew his movements, now he'll think I've been discussing him with her. Though heaven knows how he thinks I've managed that when he's got my phone.

'I am,' he says. 'Why?' He sends her a tight smile.

'That's settled. It's the Knutsford markets tomorrow. I'll pick you up at eleven o'clock, Mia.'

He tops up my glass. 'Darling, why not have more wine? It is your birthday.' I see his jaw clench. He's trying to work out how to get me out of tomorrow without coming across like a control freak.

I can see Mum has begun to sense the tension. Mum lifts her glass. 'Happy Birthday, Mia.'

The family dutifully choruses, 'Happy Birthday!'

I too raise my glass, looking at Beth and praying tomorrow really happens. It will look suspicious if he says no again.

Waiting for our desserts, Beth talks about the Knutsford markets and the wonderful cheese stalls they have. 'I adore cheese. I always spend a bloody fortune when I go. You have to try them, Mia, they're to die for. It's been ages since you went. There's lots of other foodie stalls but I always go for my cheese first.' She's rambling like she does when she's annoyed. 'I can't wait to go with you. It's been ages since we did anything together. You won't mind will you, Ricky.' She's not asking.

Zoe chips in about only eating organic cheese and on cue the rest of the family all roll their eyes. Mum says she'll join us tomorrow. 'We can grab a drink somewhere afterwards,' she says, 'a coffee or something to eat and make an afternoon of it, the three of us.' She looks a little concerned but I can't be sure it's for the reasons I'd like.

'I should imagine none of you will be fit for eating or drinking after all the tasting from the stalls. I can pick you up on my way back, Mia. I don't think I'll be long at this do, it's only a drinks thing to say hello to the new director of something or other. These things never last very long.'

I know he's lying, because from experience they always last all day — or at least that's what he tells me.

After coffee and tiny chocolates, one for each of us, we head for our rooms. On the way to the stairs, Ricky pulls me to one side near the kitchen doors. His hold on my arm is painful. 'You know what happens when I find out you've lied to me. I don't know how you've been in touch with Beth, but you're going to be sorry for deceiving me.' The kitchen door swings open and Lindy comes out. She stops abruptly and stares, catching the way Ricky is clasping my arm and his threatening stance. I notice her take it all in. She doesn't miss any of it.

She bestows a dark look on Ricky. Afraid she is about to say something to him, I hold my breath. To my relief she offers us a bright smile. 'Are you wanting your room keys? I'll fetch them for you. We're a little understaffed at the moment, most of the staff are laid up with the flu. Sorry you had to wait.' She doesn't sound sorry at all, quite the opposite.

'You American?' Ricky asks bluntly.

Without batting an eyelid, she expends a deep sigh. 'No,' she says, her voice heavy with sarcasm, 'I just watch a lot of TV. Room 280, right? Will you be having breakfast downstairs or do you want room service?'

Taken aback by her rudeness, Ricky says. 'In our room.' He snatches the key from her hand, yanks at my arm and drags me towards the stairs.

CHAPTER 5

Lindy

On Sunday I get up early. I prepare myself a small breakfast of scrambled eggs on toast. It's simple and quick. Sometimes I have Weetabix because it's even simpler. I cannot be bothered with cooking. Our refrigerator is packed with "ping ping" meals.

Last night's used coffee cup and his dirty dishes lie in the sink. It irritates me. I take a quick gulp of orange juice, spilling some down my dressing gown and wiping it with my sleeve.

After it all happened, I couldn't bear to stay in our beautiful house. Having extended our bijou home, I now wanted something smaller. Different. So, we downsized to this two up, two down modern box on the estate behind Mia.

Frank has been up and as usual, he's gone back to bed. He'll get up later and watch TV. It's pretty much all he does these days. He might spend some time in the small garden we have.

Holding my cup of tea, I look out at it through the back-door window. He's kept it looking half-decent and has cut most of the shrubs back ready for the winter frost. He's fixed the broken birdbath, too. It was overgrown with weeds and hidden by knee-high grass at one time. It's now lovingly cared for. The grass has been removed, to be replaced by honey-coloured flag-stones. The overgrown rose bushes have been pruned back hard. Frank spends all his time out there, when he's not watching TV. He told me he was doing it for me.

'I want to make it a sanctuary for you, Lindy. Somewhere you can go and relax, so you can forget all about the terrible things that have happened. I'm trying to make it good again for us.'

'Good again?' I fired back, gripping the table so I wouldn't collapse under the wave of nausea his words invoked. 'You think a garden with a few attractive plants in it is going to make it good again? How will that work exactly?'

Why doesn't he understand how bad things are for us? Why can't he understand how I feel? He wants to talk — about what? There's nothing more to say. I can't talk about it. Not anymore.

I can't talk, and I can't relax. Not here, not anywhere. Does he think that for one minute I can forget? It's all I think of. My brain is full of it, every single moment I'm awake. Every day I wake up wishing I was dead. That he was. There is no us. There never will be an us, ever.

He's coming down. I hear him on the stairs. I make myself busy, keep my eyes down. I pull a dishwasher tablet from the box under the sink and chuck it into the dishwasher.

Frank hovers in the doorway.

'Lindy?' His voice is soft, barely a whisper.

I turn towards him, rearranging my expression. I fail mis-erably. I hold my breath, knowing what he's about to say next. I cast my eyes around the kitchen, towards the front door. I need to leave before he says the words I don't want to hear.

'Frank. Don't start now.' My cup crashes down on the table, harder than I'd intended. I don't want a fight. I just want him to leave me alone.

'Lindy, we can't go on like this. We need help.' The pain in his voice resonates with the pain in my head.

Praying for him to shut up and stop talking, I close my eyes, breathe. Still, my words fly out before I have a chance to restrain them. '*You* need help, you mean.' Please. We're not going to talk about it. I can't.

'No,' he says, keeping his tone calm in an attempt to keep me from bolting like I always do. 'We both need help. Look, I've been thinking . . .' He steps forward. I know he wants to help but can't he see there's nothing he can do? There is no help.

'Really? How novel for you. You've managed to think for yourself at last. Pity you didn't do any thinking that day.' My voice trembles. My throat constricts. My breath quickens. I can't face it. Trying to block the images that rise into my mind, sharp, hideous. I'm losing it. I'm falling into that dark abyss of horror and pain. I know where this will end if I don't stop it.

He wants to say more. My face is stony. What can he say? Really, does he think I can stomach his compassion after what happened that day?

He takes a loud deep breath and releases it. He sounds like a steam train coming to a stop. I move to the door and stand, resting my head on the frame. I'm exhausted. I don't want to talk about it. I just want to forget.

'We need to forgive ourselves.' His face is a picture of misery.

I turn slowly to face him, holding the door for support.

He steps back. I stare at him, unable to speak. Then I can't help myself, the words come out, brittle. Cutting. Meant to wound. 'Forgive ourselves? *Our*selves? Really? We said we would never speak of it. Fuck you, Frank, for breaking that promise.' My tears fall freely now. I swipe them away, angrily. 'I will never forgive you. *Never*!'

I rush upstairs to the bedroom. Frank follows. He looks concerned, the sort of look you give someone who's about to run into a burning building. I grab some clothes and throw them on. All black. To match my mood. 'You know what people say about us, don't you? They say we should get over it. Not to our faces, though. It's all in their pitying looks. Get over it, like a bad cold.'

'I don't think people think that.'

'How would you know? You never go out,' I snap.

I brush past Frank in the hallway on my way out of the house. He clutches my arm as I walk past. I flinch. 'Don't touch me,' I say, yanking my arm away. 'Don't fucking touch me.'

* * *

Later in the day, I pull up opposite Mia's house just in time to see them arrive back. Ricky opens the front door and pulls her inside. His face is hard and cold. A vicious smile is playing on his lips.

Five minutes later, he emerges again. I watch him lock the front door and make doubly sure it's locked. Before he pulls out of the drive, he stops and makes a call. With my binoculars, I can see right into his car. He laughs and touches his face, his hair, the collar of his jacket. An adulterer's touch.

I decide to follow him. He heads into Knutsford and leaves his car in the big car park overlooking the green. I find a space not too far away from him, maintaining my distance.

Following him through the town, I keep my head down, pushing my way through the crowds of shoppers. The air is chill and damp and I rub my arms to try and keep warm while pedestrians bump into me. Ricky cuts through King Street and alongside Boots. I follow. He stops at the coffee shop. I suspect he's meeting someone there. My skin prickles with anticipation. I pass the coffee shop, and see him seated outside on one of the tall stools. The attractive blonde beside him is my GP, Christine Saville.

A creature of habit is our Ricky. He goes out every Sunday. I've always believed he was playing golf. I never bothered to follow him, preferring to watch Mia moving about inside the house. Sometimes I peered in through the downstairs windows. The tidiness of the house never ceased to amaze me; even on a weekend there was never a single empty takeaway carton left out. No used cups. Even the dogs' toys were neatly stacked in a corner of the kitchen.

How long has he been having this affair? I snatch a couple of photos on my phone as I walk past, hidden behind a group of mothers with their offspring in pushchairs.

Earlier, after my fight with Frank, I followed Ricky and Mia to the Sunday markets, where they met Beth. Mia appeared on edge and Ricky held her hand the entire time. Beth wasn't happy, I could see. She frowned whenever Ricky whispered something to Mia.

Determined to find out more, I "accidentally" bumped into them.

I stumbled, slamming into Ricky and forcing him to let go of Mia's hand. 'Oh, hi,' I said. 'Sorry. I'm so clumsy.' I stood between them. Each time Ricky tried to get close to Mia, I blocked him. He was beginning to get annoyed. I've noticed that whenever he gets angry he gets a little pink along the side of his neck.

As Ricky tried to edge his way closer to her, Mia gave me a tense smile. 'Oh, Lindy. Sorry, yes, I didn't recognise you for a second. How are you?' I smiled back. Ricky's petulant expression was like that of a spoiled child whose toy has been taken away.

'Great. Did you enjoy your meal and your stay in the hotel?'

'Yes, thanks. We all had a lovely time.' Her eyes flicked to Ricky, now standing behind me. She was obviously uncomfortable talking to me in his presence. I was tempted to make some comment about how clingy he was, like a leech, but I saw real fear in her eyes and thought better of it. We stood in a small group, with people knocking into us as they made for the stalls.

I could see she was sick with nerves. It irked me that he was making her feel so uncomfortable.

'Listen, I was thinking of doing more of your classes and I wanted to ask which ones were less busy. The time of day isn't a problem, I can easily change my shifts.'

'Oh, er, I've stopped. I mean I don't do them anymore. Go to the gym, I think they have a replacement. The new lady — Lucy, I think that's her name. She's very good. You'll be happy with her.' She smiled miserably.

'You've quit? Why?' I was one step short of saying, *You can't quit! What the hell am I going to do now?* I felt like giving her a good shake, like they do in those black and white melodramas on TV.

She stared at me, her eyes wide with fear and something like panic. 'I want to spend more time at home.' She reached for Ricky's hand. 'With Ricky. The job is keeping us apart.'

Ricky shouldered me out of the way, sending me crashing into one of the stalls and knocking over a stand of carefully stacked cheeses. He pulled her to his side and stood, raking his fingers through his blond hair. He was staking his claim and telling me to sod off.

I wasn't so easily dismissed. 'I thought you said you loved your job?'

'We want to spend more time together,' Mia said, her voice breaking. She looked pleadingly at Ricky.

He lifted her hand and kissed it. 'Lindy, is it? I really don't think you should be badgering my wife like this. You can find another teacher at the gym. It's only a spin class, after all.'

'Only a spin class?' I knew it wasn't anything to get annoyed about, but the way he said it infuriated me. I felt my anger begin to boil and decided I'd better make my escape.

I went straight to the gym to find out exactly what had happened. Combing my hair with my fingers, I approached the reception desk and introduced myself as one of Mia's friends. One of the personal trainers who was chatting up the reception-ist told me she'd phoned out of the blue and told them she was leaving. She gave no explanation, he said, just that it wasn't for her.

'Didn't you think that was strange?' I asked.

The receptionist shrugged. 'She sounded OK to me. She said she wanted to spend more time at home with her hus-band. I thought it was rather sweet.'

'What's sweet about it?' I asked.

She scowled at me as if I was dense, and I wanted to slap her. 'It's sweet that she wants to stop working to spend time with her husband. I think it's romantic. Her husband is well dreamy. If I was her, I'd want to spend more time with him too.' She glanced up at the PT and flashed him a smile like an advert for toothpaste.

Idiot.

In my imagination Mia and Ricky had amazing sex and exotic holidays, and fabulous dinner parties with gourmet meals and expensive wines. They'd have candles all over the house.

On holiday he would rub suncream into her smooth golden skin so she wouldn't burn. They'd travel first class. No, probably business class. I don't think they're quite rich enough for first class. When the kids were young, they'd have gone to Florida. They'd have hired a villa somewhere amazing like Captiva, maybe with friends. It's nice there. Frank and I went in the early days. It's been so long since I've thought about the good days. The memory makes me want to cry.

I grew up with a stay-at-home mom and a dad who went out to work. It was the norm in those days. Mom was big but she moved her ample frame around like it was made of gossamer. Whenever we came home from school, she was always there with a glass of milk and a sandwich. My sister and I took them outside and threw them over the fence of the grisly, bearded man with one leg who lived on the corner of our street. Then we raced to the store and had a milkshake. Old Mr Tanner, who ran the store, made us take out the garbage and sweep the floor in payment.

Later, when we'd finished playing on our bikes, we told Mom how much we'd enjoyed the sandwiches. I can't imagine what the bearded man's back yard must have looked like, with the heaps of rotting sandwiches against his fence. He never mentioned it.

Our parents were supportive, nurturing. Until I crossed the line. There was no point arguing. Mother was always right, even when she was wrong.

We had rules, my sister Ruby and I, rules that had to be followed. Oh, we wouldn't get in trouble. Mom just shouted and made us feel crap. We got used to it. We weren't beaten or locked up, just told off.

Once I was in college, I realised she was bitter about the way her life had turned out. People who are bitter and judgemental are generally conscious of their own failings. She'd had dreams of what she wanted to do with her life, but instead she got married and that was that. She always maintained she wasn't dissatisfied. But she was. I only realised it when I got older, when she ceased to be the primary focus of my life and I could see her objectively.

When I was sixteen, I came home with a new friend, Camilla. I was shocked to discover that my mom was racist and a bigot. You have to remember I grew up in the States, and in the South at that time the races never mixed, there was no diversity like there is today.

In our case the situation had never previously arisen. We'd never even thought about it and what it could mean. Camilla was mixed-race and she was beautiful. She had skin the colour of a soft suntan. I loved her unruly hair. She was tall and graceful and she was my best friend.

Camilla stayed over one night. It was a disaster. Mom ignored her, and when forced to address her she was rude. My father didn't speak to me for a month. The neighbours crossed the street whenever they saw my parents and me. Mom and Dad hadn't wanted her to stay but I dug my heels in. Because of that, our whole family was ostracised; you could cut the atmosphere with a knife.

The neighbours cold-shouldered us for a long time. I was ashamed of my mother for the way she'd behaved, and pained for how she made Camilla feel. Lamentably, Camilla was accustomed to white people treating her badly. She never stayed again. Mom refused, point-blank, to have her in the house. She had no explanation. No reasons why. Anyway, I knew why, it was as clear as blood on snow. Mom even threw away the bedding Camilla had used. My relationship with my parents was never the same after that. I couldn't forgive them for their cruelty. It was the first time I realised what an evil world we lived in.

Camilla and I remained friends, she even came to my wedding. My parents did not, because Frank is mixed-race. After I left home, we never spoke again. They never saw their grandchildren. When it happened and I needed my mother, she wasn't there for me.

My children, Gillian and Debra, are beautiful. They are my whole life. They're lucky to have been born when they were, and have never had to deal with the problems Camilla had growing up.

And there was I believing Mia and Ricky had the perfect life. Who has the perfect life? Does it even exist? Define the perfect life.

CHAPTER 6

Mia

When we arrive home from the markets, Ricky is in one of his foul moods. I rush inside and go straight upstairs. I hear him close the front door and drop his car keys in the kitchen. He puts his jacket away in the cloakroom, uses the loo and follows me up. 'Who is that dreadful woman who keeps popping up everywhere?'

'I told you, she was in my spin class.'

'No. She said she wanted to join your spin class. Who is she?' He watches me.

'Ricky, she has been to the spin class. I think she just wants to go to more of them.'

'None of your other members pop up in our lives like that. I don't like her. Get rid of her.'

I feel myself go cold. 'How can I? You have my phone.'

'You're right. I'll do it.'

'I don't know how you're going to do that, I don't have her number.' I know I'm pushing my luck.

Ricky has a way of making everything seem like it's your fault. He twists things around until you come to believe you really are to blame, so you try to compensate and dig yourself into a hole.

Then he has you. He starts to stick the knife in. Bit by bit. The food isn't right. The drink you made him has too much ice. Not enough ice. You suggest going out for a meal together. Fat chance. He's too busy. Better still, he says, *What's the point of just the two of us going out? What will we talk about? We might as well be at home.* So, a takeaway is brought in. Expensive wine? I don't think so. It's cheap plonk or beer. Flowers just because? Absolutely not. And let's not forget the sex. He's aggressive, even a little violent. If you complain that he hurts, you're ungrateful. You should be happy he still wants to shag you, because no other man will. So you lie back and pretend, tell him how fabulous it is and how wonderful he is in bed. You learn to lie; it makes your life a little easier.

'Your sister seems very interested in spending time with you all of a sudden. And how did she know I was out this morning? Been gossiping again, have you?' He picks up my phone off the bed, taps in the password and scrolls through the messages and emails. 'Have you deleted any messages?'

'How would I do that? I don't have my phone, remember?' I hesitated for just a second, but it was long enough. Ricky has noticed. He's suspicious. What if he is? What can he do? He could always kill me, but I don't for a second think he's going to go that far. It's not Ricky's style. Too messy. Too many loose ends. Not Ricky at all.

'Mia, if you have spoken out of turn about me, you know I will find out. And you also know what will happen.'

'I might have mentioned it before you took my phone away. Before you started locking me up in my house like a criminal.'

He laughs. 'Is that what it feels like?'

I ignore him. 'Why did you let me go today? I thought you said I wasn't to leave this house until I did what you asked.'

'If I'd refused to let you go, your bloody sister would've been round here like a shot and you know it. Maybe that's what you hoped for. Tut, tut, Mia, you know I'm smarter than that. Don't you worry, I've thought it all through.' I wonder how long he's been thinking it all through. He's been off with me for a while. But this is a whole new level.

Ricky was so caring in the beginning. Not long after we met I had a car accident. It was all my fault. I'd had a lot on my mind that day. I was driving down a narrow country lane far too fast when I turned a corner and found myself heading towards a tractor. I had a fleeting second to decide what to do — head-on or the stone wall. I chose the wall. The car was a write-off. As soon as Mum and Dad called him, Ricky was at my hospital bedside. He never really left. I was pregnant but I didn't lose the baby.

I thought he loved me, but I see now it was only a trap. He wanted the lifestyle and the standing my family would give him. I was the golden goose, and he wasn't going to let it slip out of his grasp. There's nobody like Ricky for charm. He soon had my family eating out of his hand. As for me, I had a feeling we weren't right for each other. I should have had the guts to say no.

He didn't wait long. He told Mum and Dad he was going to marry me just days after I came out of hospital. He told me he'd found the most wonderful house for us and had put in an offer. I would love it, he said. It was so easy to have him take charge. I'm quite indecisive at times, I would never have been able to choose a house — something Ricky was keen to point out. Later, he told me how annoying it was that I was always so passive. Anyhow, I was grateful. He did it all. He chose the furniture and the decor. The house was all ready when he moved us in. I thought it was because I was pregnant and he was concerned about the baby. How wrong I was.

The accident left me with a fractured cheekbone and some whiplash. The police said I was lucky to have come out from it alive. Ricky was very considerate. He insisted I rest. He took time off from work to look after me. My friends told me it was a bit over the top, they thought it was strange. But

I wouldn't hear a word against him. None of my friends had husbands as caring as Ricky.

He said I wasn't to drive, so he always took me to see Mum and Dad. It was true I was nervous of getting into a car again. He told me to take it easy and that in time I would be fine. He was right. Mum always said he was thoughtful.

My grandmother died five years ago. Looking back, it was around that time that he began to grow more controlling. Right from the start of our marriage, he had been the one in charge. If the girls played up or were rude to me, it was Ricky who punished them. He never hit them or anything, but would take their toys away, or stop them participating in their favourite activities. He said he loved me so much that he couldn't bear anyone being hurtful to me. But then he hit me because I couldn't control the girls. He hit me because he could. He knew no one would believe me if I told them what he did.

While Ricky was growing up his family moved from place to place. Ricky had a dictatorial father, who had been headmaster at a boys' private school. His father couldn't abide disobedience and bad timekeeping, and Ricky had to toe the line, or face punishment.

'Where do you go when you're not here?' I ask. 'You can't possibly be working all the time.' I want him to admit he has another woman. He won't, of course. It will show weakness. Ricky doesn't like to appear weak. But he is. He's a bully, and all bullies are weak. He's a bully at work and he bullies me.

'I don't need to justify myself to you.'

'Why did you pull out of the lunch I wanted to have?'

'Think I was going to leave you alone with your sister? No chance.'

'You called Mum and told her not to come along with us to the markets. She was upset. Why did you do that?'

'Why do you think? Anyway, I told her you and Beth needed time together. Obviously she didn't know I was going to be with you.'

All the time I was at the markets I kept looking around to see if any woman made eye contact with him. Nobody did. No, Ricky is careful to avoid rumours that might damage his career. Nobody likes an adulterer. The last thing he'd want is for people to sympathise with me, the cheated-on wife. He won't be able to keep it a secret for too long, though. She won't want to be kept out in the cold forever. Especially if Ricky does get the position in London he's after. She'll want to share the limelight. If she has ambitions of her own she'll want to ride on his coattails. She won't get the chance. Ricky would never let a woman outshine him. And if it does get out and he does tell Sally, there will be nowhere for him to hide. He will be vilified by his public and the press will tear him to pieces.

He keeps all my clothing, including my shoes, in the dressing room. He keeps it locked. He locks everything away so I'm forced to live in pyjamas. Without shoes I can't go out. He turns off the heating, which he controls with his app. If I override it, he knows. He stops me reading. I don't even have a magazine. He's disabled the TV.

He turns up unexpectedly during the day and gets himself a meal, allowing me just enough food to keep me alive. 'Mia, you know if you just put my name on the account, this would all stop. Why are you so stubborn?'

'Because Granny left me that money for our girls. It isn't for me. Anyway, we have plenty of money. Why do you want to deny your children their inheritance? Why do you want all that money? Why, Ricky? Why is it so important for you to control everything?' His response is swift. The crack of palm against cheek is loud in the quiet kitchen. My squeal brings Stan and Ollie into the kitchen. They look at us and whine anxiously.

Always the same futile argument that always ends the same way. More punishment. Less food and drink. I shove him aside and bend to comfort my two retrievers.

I could smash one of the windows but they're triple-glazed. I could walk out of the house in my bare feet. But he has a hold over me. Those letters.

That knowledge.

Three weeks before I met Ricky, my uncle Martin, my dad's brother, raped me. Sally isn't Ricky's, although she looks like him. To make sure, I had a paternity test when she was born. Ricky never knew Sally wasn't his until he found the letters.

It will break Dad. Martin and Dad are extremely close; there are only a couple of years between them. We're a close family. Sally would be devastated if she knew Ricky wasn't her dad. Her whole world would collapse. I won't allow that to happen. If I tell Beth about what Ricky is doing to me, she will want to know why. I could lie and say he's unstable, but there's a risk it'll all come out. It's a risk I'm not prepared to take, too many people would be hurt. I have to find another way.

Family gatherings became difficult after it happened, but I've managed to maintain my distance from Martin and make sure we're never alone together. I want to tell my dad. I have tried, but any hint that I'm unhappy in any way causes him so much pain that I give up.

At the time it happened, Dad and Martin had just gone into business together. The truth was he supported Martin by investing in a jeweller's shop in Wilmslow for him. I helped out in the shop from time to time whenever I was in between jobs. I enjoyed it at first. I learned a lot about the different gems. Martin taught me how to read a diamond by examining the facets.

He began coming on to me. So slowly I didn't read the signs. His hand on my back as I bent over the counter. Holding my hand while I looked at a jewel through the loupe. He'd lean over me, so close I could feel his breath against my neck.

I laughed it off. He was my uncle, he was just being friendly. It got worse. He offered to help me find a job, and together we looked through the adverts for vacancies. Like I said, I'm indecisive. I didn't know what I wanted to do. I'd been to university and gained a degree in English Literature. I could quote the classics and had reams of poetry off by heart. I thought I sounded clever and important. My parents didn't think I needed a serious job — after all, I would inherit more than enough to live on. But I wanted to do something with my life. I fancied living abroad for a while. Travelling. But I had no direction. Martin seemed kind, interested in my future.

That day he asked me to stay behind and help him clear out the basement. He'd hurt his back and the mess was getting on top of him. Grateful for his help with my job search, I said yes. I had no other plans for that night anyway.

He called Dad to tell him I'd be late because I was helping him clear the basement. He said he'd make sure I got home safely.

He brought us a Chinese takeaway, which we ate on our knees. It was fun sitting on the empty wooden crates sharing a bowl of noodles. Martin told me jokes, and about the interesting adventures he and Dad had had when they were young. He made me see a different side of Dad. I learned that he'd been a bit of a rebel in his youth. I liked knowing that about him. At one point he reached out and wiped some sweet and sour sauce off my lip with his finger. It made me feel awkward. I laughed it off. Then he stroked my hair, which made me shy away. He told me not to be frightened. He wasn't laughing anymore.

Suddenly the atmosphere in the room had changed. I shivered. Martin took the dirty dishes away and came back with a blanket.

'Here. You look cold. Sit closer to me and I'll wrap the blanket around us.'

'But what about the clearing up?' I looked around the room.

'Let's warm up a little first, shall we?' He pulled me towards him. I hesitated, suddenly stiff. He moved up and wrapped the blanket around us. 'You're very beautiful, you know, Mia.'

Nervous, I searched around for something to say. 'Why haven't you ever married, Uncle Martin?'

'Never found the right woman.' He pulled up the sleeve of my jumper and began gently stroking my arm. A shiver ran down my back. I was horrified to find I was getting turned on. I sat trying not to breathe as his hand travelled slowly from my arm to my breast. He squeezed. My nipples hardened at the touch and he teased them with his thumb. I wanted to get up and run away. I didn't move.

As I sat, frozen and miserable, he told me he'd always found me attractive. He said he'd never got married because he'd never found anyone as lovely as me. His hand moved around behind me and he unclipped my bra. There was no mistaking what he wanted now. What should I do? I couldn't tell my dad. Even if he believed me, it would wreck our family. My heart thumped. Now I was scared. What would he do if I pushed him away?

'I know you want this too, Mia. Let me undo your trousers.' I put my hand on my zip to stop him. He was kissing my neck. He began licking my jaw line until his tongue was inside my mouth. Involuntarily, I let out a sigh. 'I love you, Mia. You love me. Your body wants it. I can feel how wet you are.' His hand was inside my knickers, his fingers stroking, rubbing.

He sat up then and put the blanket on the floor. He laid me down upon it. Paralysed with fear and shame, I let him do what he wanted. This was all wrong. He was my uncle. He pulled his trousers off and then mine. He took off my knickers and smelled them. At that point I disconnected from my body. This wasn't happening.

'When two people love each other it's not wrong, Mia. We are meant to do this. We want each other. Look how your body wants mine.' He pushed two fingers inside me, pulled them out and sucked them. 'You taste delicious. You wouldn't be this wet if you didn't want me.'

I found my voice. 'Martin. Uncle. This isn't right. We can't—'

His fingers were under my nose. 'Smell how exquisite you are. This is love, Mia. True love. A love so powerful only we need know. No one would understand the love we have.' He raised himself above me. I found a spot on the wall above his shoulder and focused my gaze on it.

He groaned like an animal. Suddenly he was so big. I'd never felt so frightened before.

'You need a man, Mia. Like me. I will cherish you and love you.' He slid inside me. Gazing over his shoulder at the spot on the wall I saw a white beach and palm trees. I felt the heat of the sun.

When it was over, I wouldn't let him take me home. In a daze, I wandered aimlessly around the village, through the park. I didn't know what to do. My only thought was that I had to get away. I could go abroad. Yes, that's what I'd do. Go away for a long time, until Uncle Martin was dead and gone, then I might come home.

Three weeks later, I met Ricky. I knew intuitively that I was pregnant by then. I could sense the changes in my body. I knew Ricky wanted me for my money and my family's status in the county. I didn't care. I didn't want an abortion and I didn't want to bring up a baby on my own. When Ricky proposed, I accepted at once.

I don't know how long I can keep this up. He'll never agree to a divorce, not without the money. It amounts to more than our house is worth. That money is mine to give to the girls when the time is right. The last thing I want is for some mercenary man to turn their heads and get his hands on it. They need to be mature. They need to have lived enough not to be beguiled by some handsome, charismatic man. Like I was.

If there was somebody to talk to, I might see a way out. Alone, I'm lost.

Before he incarcerated me I did some research on the internet to find out what options I had. I even saw a lawyer, but was unable to explain my position, they'd only have told me to go to the police, and I don't want that. I have my family to think of.

If I divorce him, he's entitled to half the money. That's not enough for him, he wants the lot. I could tell the girls about it, hand it over to them. Except that if I did, Ricky would tell both Sally and Dad about Martin. I should have placed it in a trust long ago.

'I'm going out for a bit. You won't be able to use your laptop, I've put a security code in. Don't answer the door. I know Beth will probably try to come and see you when you don't answer your mobile. I'll send her a text to keep her happy. Remember, I'll be watching. There's a do at work that you need to attend with me next week. I want you to buy something new. I'll go to John Lewis with you. It's a good thing you're cutting down on your food. We don't want you looking fat, do we?'

CHAPTER 7

Lindy

I'm at the hotel, putting on my uniform in the lady's toilet. We don't have changing rooms or a staff room. We use the loos to dress and on our breaks, we eat our meals on a rickety old table in the corner of the kitchen that Jack has kindly provided. The benevolence of the man has no limits. The table wobbles. We have to shove wads of paper under one of the legs to keep it steady, so our food doesn't slide off onto the floor.

One of the first things I did when I came here was to insist we have somewhere to take our breaks. Until then, the staff ate standing up wherever they could find an out-of-the-way spot. You'd think I was demanding the best table in the restaurant laid out with linen tablecloths, silver cutlery and waiter service. The tight bastard. Initially, he supplied two chairs and told us to share. We now have three. I think he's too dumb to realise how much he alienates his staff.

'Jack, it's the law. You have to provide a place for us to take our breaks and sit for our meals.'

'You're always telling me what to do. In this hotel, I am the law.' He jabs his pudgy finger at my chest. He certainly has grandiose ideas of his position in the world. 'Share the chairs if there's not enough. It won't kill you to stand up and eat. Good for the digestion my mother always said.' He rubs his ample stomach as if it's a response to our demands.

'If we don't get enough chairs we'll be late back from our shifts because we'll have to wait for a seat. Is that what you want?'

His eyes grow huge. They look like billiard balls about to pop right out of his head. 'You will not be late! I will stop your money if you're late coming off your breaks.'

'Shut up, Jack. You know you can't do that. Do you want me to call the tax office and tell them you're stopping our pay? I'm sure you don't want them poking around your business.' Sometimes I think his brain doesn't work like other people's, there's no connection with his mouth. And the drivel he spouts makes me want to push him over just so I can watch him try to get back up.

Jack storms off, muttering under his breath. Like I said, he's dumb. He never remembers that I understand Spanish. 'Motherfucker yourself,' I say irritably to his retreating back.

'I don't know how you keep on working for that mean bugger,' Joanne says from the rickety table, biting into her sandwich. She's one of the waitresses. She's been here six months, and I suspect she's looking for something else. I mostly try to eat by myself. Mealtimes can be a bit of a trial, because Joanne's break time nearly always coincides with mine. I think she plans it that way. I can't move away because of the chair situation. To forestall her chat, I call my daughter, Gill. She doesn't answer, so I listen to her voicemail and hang up without leaving a message. I take a deep breath and let it out slowly. It's a habit I have, and I can't seem to break it.

'I can't be bothered to go anywhere else,' I tell her, biting into my own sandwich. 'It's handy. I don't give a shit about Jack and he knows it. If I went someplace else, I'd have to watch myself.' That's the truth of it. I can be as rude and snappy to him as I like, and all he does is scowl and mutter

Bloody Americans. Jack doesn't know why I'm like this, but he knows I walk under a dark cloud.

'Why do you phone your daughter every day at the same time? Doesn't it annoy her? Why not call her at some other time? Anyhow, I'm not staying here much longer. I've spoken to Jack about docking my pay. Each month he gives me a little less money. He says I've been late clocking in. I don't know how he works that out, it's all electronic. I'm never late.'

I don't really care about her problems but neither do I like injustice, and Joanne is a good worker. She's never late. She's never mentioned my calls before. I wonder what made her ask today. I shrug, making a mental note to call Gill in private in future.

Jack is always taking money off me, too. Every month we argue about it and he gives it back. 'Why you bother me so much? It's a couple of quid,' he snarls. 'All this extra paperwork. Lindy, you need to get a life and stop worrying about the little things. Take some extra food instead. Go. Leave me alone. I not log back in to the computer. You know what I have to do? I have to redo your payslip. It just gives me more work.'

'You're a thief, Jack Torres. I don't care if it's fifty pence. It's mine and I want it. It's not like it's a genuine mistake — you take the money on purpose.'

Huffing and puffing, he waves me feebly away. 'I not do it, Lindy.' He throws me the extra money in coins. I like pissing him off. Rattling his cage is one of my few pleasures in life. I think he knows I wouldn't call the tax office. Jack Torres knows I don't give a shit about anything much. In a peculiar sort of way, we get on. Neither of us seems to like the other much, yet in a twisted fashion we do. I'd like to tell him what I really think of him but I don't. If I do lose this job, I doubt I'll find another. So I zip it.

When my shift finishes, I head for the gym. I bought some new gym gear before I knew Mia had left so I didn't stand out in my tatty leggings. I go mostly in the hope of finding out more about her, and in case anyone tells me the real reason why she left. Mia loved her job. I can't believe she left it to stay at home.

I manage to get hold of her phone number by handing the love-sick receptionist thirty pounds, and ring Mia from my car. Her voice breathy and edgy, she says, 'Who is it?'

'Mia? It's Lindy. Are you OK? You sound odd.'

'Oh, hi, Lindy.' There's a pause. Probably she's wondering who the fuck Lindy is. Then she remembers. 'How did you get my number?' I hear a door closing, then the sound of running water. She's talking to me in the bathroom with the shower going, whispering, as though she doesn't want anyone to hear. I plug my finger in my other ear to hear her better.

'Lindy, I need help. Ricky has taken my phone off me, but I just heard it ringing. He hid it in the wardrobe and didn't turn it off, thank God.'

'What? Why?'

'I don't have time. I need your help. Listen to me, please.'

'Help? With what?'

'Call my sister. Write her number down.'

'Why not text it?'

'I can't. I don't have my phone, just the house phone. Quick, write it down.'

I cast around for a pen and paper. Why is there never any paper around when you need it? I pull a shop receipt from my handbag and scribble the number down. 'What do you want me to say to your sister? Mia, what's happened? What's going on?'

'I have to go.'

The line goes dead.

* * *

When I walk into the spin class, Lucy is chatting to some of the regulars. She tells them Mia's left and she'll be taking the class. There's an unoccupied bike at the front and two at the back. I introduce myself and head for the back.

Lucy threads her way through the rows of bikes towards me. 'Lindy?'

'Hi.'

'You're still a newbie, aren't you? Why not use the bike at the front, where I can keep an eye on you?'

'Thanks, but I'd rather sit at the back.' I don't want to stand out, which is exactly what is happening now.

Lucy smiles brightly. 'Nonsense.' She takes hold of my hand and leads me firmly back to the front. 'I'll look after you. Besides, it's better at the front, you don't see the others so you don't worry if you're not keeping up.'

Rather than make a scene, I give in. I slip my foot into the pedal stirrup and make sure it's secure. I adjust my seat and place my water bottle in the holder in front of the handlebars. 'OK. I'm good to go,' I say with a confidence I'm not feeling.

Lucy puts her headset on and the screen behind her comes alive. We're cycling through a forest. 'OK. Are we all ready?' Abruptly, the music starts. It's deafening. I feel as if I'm at a rave without the drugs or the flashing lights. Lucy counts down: 'Five, four, three, two, one — let's go!' Oh God, now I need to pee. I hope I can make it through the session without having an accident.

* * *

Afterwards, I nip across to the pub over the road to grab a bite to eat and recover. I was this close to wetting myself during that damn spin class. Love's young dream is behind the bar. I wonder if he'll remember me. Probably not. I give it a shot anyway. 'Hey, remember me?' I give him my great all-American smile and lift my hair off my neck the way Mia did that day. He stares at me as if I have pulled off my wig to reveal a bald head. Come on, I'm not as bad as all that.

'Er, no.'

'Never mind, Casanova.' I grab the menu off the bar. 'I'll have a BLT with fries and a glass of orange juice.'

'Who's Casanova?'

I wait a moment to see if he's joking. He's not. 'Well it's not you, buddy, that's for sure. I'll take the table over there.' I point to the table furthest away from the bar and make my way over.

When he brings over my order, I ask him, 'Remember that blonde you had the hots for a couple of weeks ago? Comes in every Monday evening with her girlfriends?'

He thinks for a moment, squinting as though he's delving into the deep recesses of a vast brain. Then his face brightens, and I can almost see the lightbulb going on inside his head. 'Oh yeah, I remember her. Hot MILF.' He gives a lecherous grin that's certainly not for me.

I roll my eyes. 'Yeah, her. Has she been in this week?'

'No, not seen her. Shame, she didn't half do it for me. What a bod.' He shakes his hand like he's burnt it. 'Hot. Sooo hot.'

'Get a grip, Casanova. By the way, you forgot my fries.'

'Who's this Casanova guy anyway?' he asks in all seriousness. 'You must have me mistaken for him.'

I bite into my BLT. 'Fries?'

He saunters off back to the kitchen, his jeans so far down his hips that his underpants are showing. Such a skanky look.

That's odd. Mia hasn't missed a Monday since I began stalking her.

A woman and what I presume are her two grown-up daughters walk in, all chattering at once. Still chattering, they grab a table. I watch while they order. They laugh. One of the girls shows her mum something on her phone, and the three of them giggle. They're about the same age as my girls, and of a similar build.

I'll tell you about my two girls now, it's about time you heard. You should know something about the only bright light in my dark world.

Gilly's the eldest. She's smart. She works in a leading PR company, in charge of some of their principal accounts. You know — like celebrities. She can't say much, of course, but we get a little gossip if we squeeze her.

Debra is very creative. She works for a design agency — toys. I know it sounds silly, but someone has to do it. She's always full of ideas. I don't know who she inherited that from. They've sold many of their ideas to big toy manufacturers in America like Hasbro and Mattel, Fisher Price, Polly Pocket.

My girls are smart and sassy. They'll go places. I wish they were here with me now. We'd be laughing and giggling like the three over there. Gillian looks like me — when I was half-decent, that is. She doesn't look like me now, thank God. I sigh. I must go and visit them soon. They're too busy to come to us, they're young with full lives. Busy lives.

CHAPTER 8

Mia

Finally, I realise that Ricky is enjoying his transformation into a monster. He's getting off on the cruelty. It's making him reckless.

Thinking back, I realise how stupid and pathetic I've been in allowing it to get this far. I should have left him soon after we married, when he first started playing his emotional games. I stayed then because of my parents. They adore him. He never puts a foot wrong with them. And now he's worked his charm on the girls. Mother hates the very idea of divorce. She keeps telling me that now she's getting older, she's relieved that I have someone who will take care of me after they're gone. Mum likes to have everything in order. 'All the boxes ticked, Mia,' she says. 'Deal with things when they happen. It makes life easier.'

The first time my mother seemed to have any doubts about Ricky was at my birthday meal at the Dahlia, when he stopped me sitting with Beth. Previously, he had always given into Mum, because he needed her as an ally.

I'm frightened and angry that I've put myself in this impossible position. I should have destroyed those letters. Why did I even write them in the first place? I had been reading an article about how writing down your problems and feelings helps you to deal with them. Fine, but I needn't have kept them. Even if Ricky hadn't found them, what if I had died and Sally and Annie came across them? They would have been devastated.

Stan and Ollie trail after me around the kitchen. I need to get out of this house and speak to someone. It's insane being kept locked up like this. When I asked him for a set of keys he said, 'When you decide to do as I ask, I'll give them to you. Until you do, you'll be staying inside. And don't go blabbing to anyone about our private business. We don't want people gossiping about us, do we? I'm sure you don't want us to be one of *those* couples.'

'How is that going to happen if I'm locked up in here?'

He won't break me. He might do me physical harm but he will never break my spirit.

He's upstairs now, having his shower. There's only enough food for his breakfast. He's put locks on the pantry. Only he has the key. I'm starving. Last night he gave me fruit for dinner, an apple and some blackberries, while he made himself a curry. He gave the leftovers to the dogs and threw the rest away. Knowing I'll be punished for it, I grab the slice of bread he has put out for his breakfast, along with a couple of eggs. I make scrambled eggs. I eat the lot. I'm putting the dishes in the dishwasher when I hear him leave the bathroom.

I need to let the dogs out, but I can't open the doors. 'It's OK, boys, Ricky will be down soon, and then you can go out.' I bend down and stroke them and they look at me with their sad brown eyes. 'I wish you understood what I'm saying.' They jump up and push me over. I sit on the floor, hugging them to me. 'I might be sharing your food soon, if he doesn't give me more to eat. You won't mind, will you?' Stan gives me another head butt.

Ricky is standing at the kitchen door, watching us. I clamber to my feet, brushing dog hairs off my pyjamas. 'I need the keys so I can let them out,' I say.

'Here.' He tosses me the keys. Catching hold of them, I stare at him for a moment in surprise. As soon as the door is open, Stan and Ollie race out and turn in circles before relieving themselves. 'What are we going to do about them, Mia?'

'Do about them? What do you mean?' My voice falters.

'Well, I can't leave you with the keys. Maybe we should put them in kennels until you come to your senses.'

'They've never been in kennels. They'll hate it. They won't understand what's going on.'

'We'll re-home them then.'

'No!' I think fast, the panic building in my chest. 'Why can't we leave them with Beth like we always do when we go away?'

'Beth? And have her asking questions? No, it's the kennels or we find them another home.'

He can't do this. They're all I have left. 'I know. We can tell Beth I've developed asthma and the doctor's told me I shouldn't be around them until it settles.'

'Settles? What settles? Your stubbornness?'

'Look, Ricky. I'll call Beth now. She can come over and pick them up while you're here, so you can make sure I don't say anything to her. Nothing can happen while you're here, can it?'

He nods. It's only a temporary respite, I know. He's going to use the dogs as leverage. No battle with Ricky is won this easily.

'Make the call and smile while you speak to her. We don't want her picking up anything untoward. Do we? I see you've eaten my breakfast.'

He gives me my phone. I make the call, hand it back to him and wait for what he will do next.

'Excellent. Now, when she arrives, I want you to be all smiles. Act loving towards me and don't go off together, do you hear? Don't think you're not getting away with eating my breakfast either.'

Glad that Stan and Ollie will be with Beth, I smile tentatively at him. I must think of some way to let Beth know I need her help.

'What if she asks to speak with me alone? I can't say no.'

'You can, Mia, and you will.'

When Beth arrives, I greet her with a warm smile. I roll my eyes to indicate what I think of the doctor's orders.

'This is so out of the blue,' she says, kissing me on the cheek and marching into the house.

Ricky is crouched in the kitchen petting the dogs and making a big show of regret at being parted from his dear pets. 'Thank you for taking them off our hands, Beth. We're both really cut up about this. But Mia's health is the most important thing, isn't it?' He smiles sadly.

'I suppose.' Beth looks from me to Ricky. 'I didn't think you were that fond of the dogs, Ricky.'

'That's how much you know about me. I love these dogs as much as Mia does. I mean, who wouldn't?' He wraps his arms around Ollie. Ollie wriggles out of his embrace and comes to my side. Stan follows. They sit either side of me as if we're posing for an old oil painting called something like "companionship".

'Are you sure you don't mind, Beth? I don't know how long it'll be for.'

With her back to Ricky, Beth bends down and strokes the dogs, looking up at me suspiciously. 'What brought the asthma on?'

Smiling like Ricky told me to, I go over and stand at his side. 'They don't know. Sometimes it can happen with the menopause.'

Beth frowns. 'The menopause? I've never heard that one before. Trust you to get something no one else has.'

'Are you disputing the doctors, Beth?' Ricky wraps an arm around my shoulder, digging his fingers into my flesh. It's all I can do not to cry out.

'Not at all, Ricky. Don't worry, Mia, they can stay with me as long as you like and you can always come visit.'

'That'll be great, yes I will, thanks,' I say. He'll never let me, of course, but I can't help hoping.

'Darling that's not going to be sensible, is it? I think for the time being it will be best for you to keep away from dogs if it's them causing the problem.'

After Beth leaves, I'm at a loss as to how to go about my new role as housekeeper, cook and bottle-washer. It never bothered me in the past. When the girls were little, I quite enjoyed being at home and doing the mundane chores. Being with them was all the satisfaction I needed. After they left, I rattled around this large house feeling trapped. Little did I know what being trapped really meant.

Trying to get into mainstream employment was impossible. In fact, as I soon discovered, it was impossible. Having gone straight from university to marriage and babies, I'd never had a job. I wasn't qualified for anything. I had no office experience. I had an interview with a recruitment agency in which I was asked if I was proficient in Excel. I'd never even heard of it.

I did lie to one recruitment agency. The next day they called and sent me for an interview, which I lied my way through. I was feeling pretty pleased with myself until they asked me to do some proficiency tests. That was the end of that job.

After that, I gave up on office work. Having talked to my PT at the gym, I decided to train as a PT myself and to my surprise, found that I was good at it.

Sighing, I stare down at the sink, where a single cup sits waiting to be washed. Ricky has left the kitchen. No doubt he's spying on me through the cameras.

The landline rings, making me jump. I thought he'd disconnected it. Lying bastard. I could have called someone — Beth. It sits on the windowsill, its shrill ring reverberating through the house like a seagull on the beach wall. I stare at it. Should I pick up the receiver? Will Ricky burst in and stop me? I make my mind up, throw the tea towel down and snatch it up.

'Hello?'

'Mia? Hi, it's Lindy. Thank God I've got hold of you. I've been trying for ages but your phone keeps going to voicemail. Are you OK? I think I took Beth's number down wrong.'

'I, er . . .' I don't know what to say to her. *Help? Help me,
Lindy. Please, he's starving me to death so he can get hold of my money.*
I keep my eyes on the kitchen door. Dare I tell her?

'You're not ill, are you? Can I do anything? I've been
round too, but you're never in.'

How does she know where I live? I know she's a bit pushy
but in an odd way I kind of like her. 'No, I'm not ill.'

The kitchen door opens. Then Ricky is by my side, smiling, eyebrows raised. 'Darling, who is it?'

'Lindy,' I whisper. He scowls.

On the other end of the line Lindy is still talking, asking
if I'm OK, calling my name.

'Why is she phoning you here? How did she get your
number?' His tone is calm and reasonable. He won't make a
scene while she's still on the line. 'Have you taken your medication, Mia? I didn't see you do it this morning.'

I frown at him. What medication? I'm about to ask when
he takes the phone from my hand. 'Good morning, Lindy.
This is Ricky, Mia's husband. We met at the hotel, if I'm not
mistaken, and at the markets. Is there something I can help
you with?'

'There is. I want to speak with Mia.'

'Sorry, Lindy. She's left the room now. Gone to take her
medication.'

I stand beside him, listening to Lindy bombard him with
questions. Ricky neatly deflects every one of them. To listen
to him, he's an adoring husband, seeing me through an acute
attack of asthma. While he speaks, he'll be trying to work out
how Lindy got our home number. I have no idea, unless they
gave it to her at the gym. His grip on my arm is like a vice. It
tightens. His tone has become sharp. Does he really think he
can keep everyone away forever? Someone will want to see me.
When they can't, they'll ask questions. Beth, for one, won't be
put off by his stupid story about asthma.

How smoothly the lies roll off his tongue. I remember the
day I found out about his affair. It was about a month ago. I

had left the gym earlier than usual and drove into Manchester to do some shopping. It was Sally's birthday and I wanted to get her some of her favourite perfume. Bloody expensive, she never buys it herself, always asks for it as a gift. They only sell it in Selfridges. I parked up and bought the perfume. On my way back to the car, I decided to grab a coffee to go.

As I made my way down Deansgate towards Starbucks, I passed a small Turkish restaurant. I forget the name. They had a fixed-price menu on a sandwich-board on the pavement, and I stopped for a moment to look at it. That's when I saw him, seated at a table with an attractive blonde. They were holding hands. I was sure I recognised her, but I couldn't put a name to her face. They were leaning towards each other, their faces inches apart. They looked so intimate. A couple exited the restaurant and barrelled into me, forcing me to move away. I walked off, telling myself I must be mistaken. Ricky wasn't even supposed to be here, he was in London, I thought. He said he was going to see his agent about a new opportunity that had come up. I stood in the middle of the pavement, undecided. Oh, God, I didn't want to look again but I had to know. Telling myself it was probably someone who looked like him, I walked slowly back and peered inside. If he'd looked up he would have seen me with my face pressed against the window. He didn't. His eyes never left her face. Nauseous with shock, I wandered off through the crowds of shoppers, lost in a whirlwind of conflicting emotions.

'No,' Ricky was saying, 'the coffee morning will be cancelled for the foreseeable future. I didn't know you came. I did send a text to Mia's friends, but it appears you're not in her contacts.'

'I'd like to speak to Mia, please,' she says.

He puts his hand over the mouthpiece.

'Ricky, give me the phone, please. I want to speak to her.' I grab hold of the receiver. He grasps my wrist and squeezes, hard. With a 'Goodbye, Lindy,' he hangs up and unplugs the phone from the wall socket.

'What have I told you?'

'This is becoming ridiculous,' I say. 'People are going to start coming to the house if they don't hear from me.'

He pulls my mobile from his pocket. 'Ah, but there's always texts. I've made it perfectly clear that you are not to speak to anyone. I am watching you. I will know who comes to the door and I will make sure none of your friends gets inside. I'm warning you, Mia. Cross me and I will tell Sally everything.'

If I find those letters and burn them, he won't have any proof. As soon as the thought enters my mind, I realise how futile that is. It's too late now. Ricky is always one step ahead. But I will find a way. He is not going to destroy my family.

'I know what you're thinking,' he says. 'The letters. Well, I don't need them. A paternity test will do the job a lot better.'

He's right, of course.

'Because you ate my food and spoke to that stupid woman without my permission, you can stay in the pantry for the rest of the day.'

'What?'

He takes hold of my arm and pulls me through to the kitchen.

'No. You can't, Ricky. What if I need the loo? Stop this. I'm not going in the pantry.' I try to pull my arm away but he presses his fingers into the underside of my wrist, crushing the nerve. The pain sends me to my knees.

He takes the key from his pocket, unlocks the door, picks me up and throws me inside. 'You'll just have to hang on, won't you?'

I bang on the door furiously. 'Ricky, don't do this. Don't! Don't leave me in here. Please!'

'Will you do what I want?'

I clench my fists.

'I thought not. I will break you, Mia. Don't doubt it. I'll be back later.'

CHAPTER 9

Lindy

John Lewis is packed. There must be a sale on. I hate shopping at the best of times. I particularly detest it when I'm forced to wade through crowds of people wandering around like zombies looking for a bargain.

People just buy stuff because it's in the sale, not because they need it. Some people are addicted to sales. They get up at silly o'clock and queue just to get something a bit cheaper. Why? Why go to all that trouble? All I wanted was something new and a bit fashionable to wear to Mia's coffee morning — I mean, I could hardly turn up in my normal attire with all her glamorous friends there. But that's cancelled now, anyway, which is odd. I can't remember the last time she cancelled a coffee morning. Still, now I'm here, I thought, I might as well buy myself something new. It's not often I get the desire to spend money on new clothes. Seeing all the shoppers, I wish I hadn't bothered.

Ricky sounded odd on the phone. I got the impression he didn't like me. No surprise there, but he wouldn't let me talk to Mia, which *was* peculiar. I heard her in the background asking for the phone but he seemed to be ignoring her. Then there was a squeal, like someone in pain. Had he hurt her, again like at the hotel? Surely not. I thought that might have been a one off. He's usually all over her like a rash. I'd hate that amount of attention. I'd suffocate. Christ, just the thought of Frank smothering me with love brings me out in a cold sweat. Some men think it gives them power over a woman. Makes them feel strong, protective of the poor little thing. I know he thinks I'm pushy. So what? Mia reached out to me, we have something special now. It's only natural that I pursue it and that I'm concerned about her. What the hell is really going on in the Hicks household?

I flick through the racks of clothes, with no idea what I'm looking for. Nothing too showy anyway. To be honest, I have plenty of things that are perfectly suitable. I don't wear them now. I haven't been clothes shopping for a long time. Gillian would know what to look for. Pulling my mobile out of my handbag, I find her name in my contacts. My finger hovers over the dial button then I drop it back inside. I can find an outfit on my own.

Twenty minutes later, I've lost the will to live. I grab hold of a passing sales assistant and ask for her help. I must have grabbed her too hard because she winces, and the happy, "I'm here to help" smile disappears from her face.

I'm in the dressing room now, four outfits hang behind the door, kindly sourced by Vicky, the sales assistant. Vicky has pink hair. She's younger than me and prettier — no surprise there — slimmer and full of enthusiasm. She clearly likes a bit of a joke because some of the dresses are a size ten. Was I ever that enthusiastic? I can't remember. I have a nagging feeling that I had something important to do today besides shopping. I can't remember that either. Christ, my brain is turning to mush. Yesterday, the phone rang while I was in the middle of a transaction at the hotel. I picked it up and was about to speak when, to my horror, I couldn't remember the name of the hotel. It was gone. Just like that. A blank. Embarrassed,

I put the phone down. 'Line's gone dead,' I muttered to the customer, and resumed the transaction.

I can't take my eyes off Vicky's hair, it's such an unusual colour — shocking pink. She's shorter than me. I peek at her roots. Perfect. Must be a wig. I might get one and wear it to work, see what it does to Jack. I picture his stunned face when I walk in with vivid pink hair. It might make him actually smile for once.

Gilly would tell me to go for it. She's not one to hold back on ideas like that. In her office there's a mixed bag of people. You'd think a PR company in London would be conservative but not a bit of it. She sends me short videos so I see the lively social environment she spends her days in.

Debra's place is a little less unconventional. Although the creative team all dress casually, the rest are more traditional. The staff at Gilly's PR company dress to shock: *Look at me, hire me, see how out there I am.*

Before Gilly and Debra moved away, we shopped together all the time. We'd do lunch and spa days. The girls loved the spa days. They'd surprise me with "wowchers" for spa days in fabulous country houses and their vicious masseurs. I miss all that. They're too far away now, and their lives have moved on.

'If you require any help with the clothes just give me a shout, Mrs Villas. I'll be at the entrance to the changing rooms.'

'I'll be OK, but thanks anyway,' I say, wondering what she'll say when I burst the zippers on the size ten outfits she's chosen for me. My face feels stiff. I realise I haven't smiled in a very long time.

Frank tells me to smile more. It always makes me want to punch him in the mouth. He says I should smile at work, out walking, shopping for groceries. I picture myself grinning inanely — I'd look like I was mentally impaired. 'I don't want to bloody smile all the time,' I say. 'Why do you think that is?' He sighs wearily and goes back to the shabby couch or his zen garden. He never answers back. He's a coward, you see. A sissy. A bollockless, spineless bastard. In the mirror I catch my lip twitching. That's all it does. Pity Vicky didn't catch me smiling, because I doubt there's another where that came from. Frank and I weren't always like this, you know. We just got stuck together through circumstances beyond our control.

I turn back to the task before me. Everything Vicky has brought in for me is too small. I'm not a ten. Why in the world did she think I was? Didn't she even look at me? I started out on this shopping trip full of hope that a new outfit would somehow make me feel better. So much for that.

Exasperated, I fling the skirt into the corner. The mirror is horribly unflattering. They do that in department stores. They should invest in flattering mirrors; they'd sell more clothes that way.

I stand in my knickers and bra staring at myself in the mirror. My belly is fuller than it was before the menopause. I hate carrying the extra pounds but I can't dredge up the will to shed them. I have tried, but after a day or two I'm asking myself what's the point. Who gives a fuck anyway. I'm tired a lot, too. Bone-achingly tired. All I want is to sleep. I get home from work exhausted, but that's when my brain fires up. At home there's little to distract me from my thoughts. Work is good; it keeps me busy and stops me thinking. At home, there's just Frank, the lightning rod to all my thoughts. Bastard.

My body is a wondrous thing. It has lasted years without giving me any trouble, whatever I've done to it. I've been healthy, fit and strong. I've never broken anything. I touch the fine threads that line my stomach and thighs, the stretch marks my babies left as a reminder. I loved being pregnant, the sensual feeling of carrying another living being inside me. I would lie in the bath, my belly bursting through the surface of the water, watching a tiny foot or hand push up from within. Me, Lindy, was protecting that tiny life. She needed me to survive, and I needed her.

Before my girls were born, I never gave a thought to unconditional love. I didn't even know what it meant. You don't when you're childless or single. Your desires are all for yourself, your aspirations are all centred on you. Nothing wrong with that, of course. You have to look out for yourself in this world. A child alters all that. You barely know it's happening until suddenly there's something more important than you. I think of my girls every single moment of every day and I worry about them. This world is a cruel and dangerous place.

'Thanks, Vicky, but none of them are right for me,' I say, handing over the clothes. I don't know why I'm even in this store, wasting my time and money just to make myself acceptable.

CHAPTER 10

Mia

When Ricky opens the pantry door, I'm lying curled up in a ball, asleep. I've no idea what the time is. I'm dizzy and thirsty, hungry and desperate for the loo. The light in the kitchen hurts my eyes.

I've been cooped up in the dark for hours. When he heaves me to my feet, my legs give way. He bends down. 'Know how long you were in there? Eight hours.' I don't respond, my whole being focused on getting to the downstairs toilet in time.

When I've finished, I make my way unsteadily to the kitchen. I grab a glass, fill it with water from the tap and drink it down. I want more, but I know not to drink too much in one go. I take a paracetamol from the kitchen drawer and swallow it with some water.

'You didn't think I'd keep you in there that long, did you?' Ricky says, watching me. 'This is only the tip of the iceberg, Mia. Things will only get worse if you continue to disobey me.'

'Can I eat something, please?' I notice a packet of chocolate biscuits next to his cup of tea and reach out for it. Ricky snatches it away.

'I'm surprised at you, Mia. You never used to be so stubborn.'

'And you never used to be so cruel.'

He lowers his voice. 'Hungry, are you?'

'Very.' My voice trembles. Despite my resolve, I can't stop the tears. When he locked me in the cupboard this morning, I believed I had the strength to see it through. It was only a few hours, but already I feel weak and beaten. Scared he'll put me back inside, I make for the kitchen door.

'Where are you going?'

'I'm leaving. I'm getting out of this house and away from you.'

'Brave words, Mia. How exactly are you going to do that?' He comes closer. 'I could kill you and make it look like an accident. Have you thought about that?'

'I have, but you won't. It will take too long for you to get your hands on the money, by which time maybe someone will have found out about your girlfriend.'

'So, you know about that, do you? Well, there's not a lot you can do about it, is there, what with you being locked in here.'

'You'll go to prison for this,' I say with more confidence than I feel.

'I don't think so. Who's to know? Only you and me. I'm not going to tell anyone, am I, and you know what'll happen if you try. Besides, it will be your word against mine. Me, the TV personality, loved by the world — including your family, don't forget. You? You're nobody. And you have no proof to back you up.'

'Who is she?'

He raises an eyebrow. 'Wouldn't you like to know.'

'Not really.' I shrug. 'I'm actually sorry for her and how disappointed she'll be when she finds out what a monster you are.'

He moves towards me and drags me over to the kitchen table. 'Sit. I'm going to feed you.'

I look at him suspiciously. 'What?'

'I have to. Otherwise, you'll get too thin and people will notice.'

I sit at the table wondering what I'll be allowed to eat, hoping it's more than a piece of fruit or a slice of toast.

'It's a bit like being in *Big Brother*, isn't it?' he says conversationally. 'Stuck in the house with me watching you all the time. I must say your sister took the story about the asthma very well, didn't she? I expected her to ask more questions, but she swallowed it, just like that.'

I wonder how long he has been mulling this over. Does *she* know, the blonde woman? Is *she* in on it? 'What exactly is your plan? Is it to drive me slowly mad with your mind games? Is that it?' He won't. I won't let him. No man is going to mess with my head.

'Now there's an idea. If you're mad, I can get power of attorney. Then I won't need you to put my name on the account. But that's messy. It takes too long, and you'd end up in a madhouse. I wouldn't recommend that, Mia. Getting out of those places is impossible once you're in.'

Even if I did get out and told Beth everything, or Lindy, would they even believe me? And what if he's working on something right now? Maybe he's speaking with them — the doctors. How can I be sure that's not what he's doing? The thought makes my blood run cold.

The bunch of keys is lying on the table. I could grab them and run. They're almost within reach.

I have to escape now before I get too weak. He puts a plate of food in front of me — strips of chicken and a small portion of steamed vegetables, the sort you can microwave in a couple of minutes. I hesitate wondering if he means to take it away from me as soon as I pick up the fork.

'Eat up, Mia. Enjoy it, it's the only meal you'll be getting for quite a few days.'

I stare at the food, fighting the urge to throw it in his face. I'll tackle him to the ground, snatch the keys and run . . . I pick up my knife and fork and begin to eat, savouring every last morsel. It tastes exquisite.

When I finish, he takes the plate away and puts a slice of buttered toast in front of me. It's slathered with Marmite. 'Come on, Mia, eat up.'

'That Marmite's going to make me incredibly thirsty.'

He smiles. 'I know.'

I'm determined not to eat the toast. I throw it at him. It lands on his chest, the Marmite leaving a sticky brown mark on the white shirt.

The smile disappears. 'You're going back in the cupboard for that. Ungrateful bitch.'

'No! I won't! I leap up from the table and race out of the kitchen.

'I can and I will and you will eat the bread.' He picks it up off the floor where it landed and, holding it out, saunters towards me. I am at the front door, pulling at the handle, knowing it won't budge. I run around the lounge, trying the locks on all the windows.

'Eat the bread, or I will force it down.'

Suddenly dizzy, I make a grab for the window ledge. I feel nauseous. What was in that food? I sway on my feet, feeling weaker and weaker. We both turn at the sound of a car pulling up outside. Through the window, I see Lindy get out. I bang on the glass with all my remaining strength. Ricky grabs me around the middle and starts tugging me backwards. I seize the curtain in one hand and pound the glass with the other. Lindy is looking over. She's heard the sound and is trying to see where it's coming from. Ricky yanks harder, and the curtain comes away from its hooks. Hanging onto it for dear life I scream, 'Lindy! Lindy, help me! Help!' My grip loosens on the curtain, and Ricky drags me away from the window, onto a small two-seater sofa in an alcove just off the room. I sink into the cushions, all my strength gone. I'm sleepy, can't keep my eyes open. When I try to speak, my words come out slurred. Ricky crouches in front of me and pushes the bread into my mouth, making me gag. He pulls back my head and makes me drink water. I can't help swallowing. Through the fog in my head I seem to hear the doorbell. Try as I might, I can't lift my head. There are voices, they sound distant. I try to speak but all I can do is mumble.

Drifting, unable to move, I hear them talking — Ricky and someone else. I try to speak but the words won't come out. There is the scent of perfume. Someone is stroking my hair, it's a gentle touch, it can't be Ricky.

When I wake up I'm in bed, Ricky beside me, holding a cup to my lips. It's hot — black coffee. I'm so thirsty, I want water. I manage to croak, 'Water.' He hands me a glass. I gulp it down too fast and immediately throw up. He removes the soiled cover and cleans me up, wiping my face gently, telling me not to worry, that it isn't good for me to get upset.

'There. That's just what I wanted to avoid, Mia. You need to drink slowly.' His voice is tender. I look away from him for a moment, wondering what new tactic this is. There, in the dim-ly-lit bedroom, I see a figure seated in the chair by the window.

'Now, Mia. Lindy is here to see you. She's been very worried since she saw you babbling that time, when you passed out, so she's come back to check on you. Are you up to seeing her, darling?'

'Lindy?'

Ricky takes hold of my hand and squeezes it. 'Come on, Mia, at least say hello. Lindy was so worried about you she got the idea I was stopping people from coming to see you. Hadn't you better tell her she's got it wrong?'

I must still be asleep, I think, and this is all a dream. Ricky would never have let Lindy inside the house, let alone into my bedroom. She stands up and comes towards me, smiling. She really is here. I struggle to raise myself up. I can talk to her. She can help me. Did Ricky say she saw me collapse? How long ago did that happen? I've no idea what day it is, or what time.

'Mia, darling, you must speak to Lindy, otherwise she's going to think badly of me. We wouldn't want that, would we?' He squeezes harder.

I lie back, silent. He fluffs the pillows, helps me to sit up, making sure I'm comfortable. He hands me the coffee, which is now practically cold. 'Come along, darling, drink some of this. It will wake you up a bit. Fancy taking too many sleeping pills. Silly ninny, you knocked yourself out.' He puts the cup to my lips but I close them tight. Last time he gave me coffee, I passed out.

'Lindy, suppose you sit on the bed with her and I'll sit in the chair. You two can chat then, and Mia can tell you she's perfectly safe and there's nothing to worry about. Maybe you can get her to drink the coffee.'

'How are you feeling, Mia?' Lindy stares hard at me. I notice that she's trying to sit with her back to Ricky, but he's positioned his chair on the other side of the bed, facing her. Meanwhile I'm coming to my senses. He's thought this through. She must have come back and insisted on seeing me. I remember now; she was in the drive and I was banging on the window, calling out to her. I didn't think she'd seen me. I must have been wrong.

'Not great. My head is sore and I'm confused. I'm hungry.'

'Fetch her something to eat, will you, Ricky?' Lindy says. He doesn't move. He sits, his fingers steepled and his chin resting on the tips. 'Hello? Can you get Mia some food? She's hungry. No need to worry, I'll be with her.'

'I don't think that's a good idea. She's been sick. She can eat later, when her stomach has settled.'

Lindy glares at him. 'Listen, if she feels hungry, she's well enough to eat. Don't be an ass. Go and get her some food.'

Reluctantly, he gets out of his chair. Before he leaves the room, he leans over and breathes in my other ear, away from Lindy, 'One word, and it's over for Sally.' He kisses me and straightens up. 'Lindy, perhaps you'd like a coffee?'

I look at her, afraid he might tamper with her drink. But Lindy doesn't seem to notice my expression. 'Sure, that'd be great. No milk, please, I'm allergic.'

But before I have time to gather my thoughts, Ricky's back. 'So sorry, Lindy, I'm going to have to ask you to leave. Mia's mother just called. She's very worried about her darling daughter and she's on her way over. I need to help Mia get herself presentable.' He puts a hand on her back and starts to usher her towards the door.

'No worries, I can stay and help,' she says blithely, moving away from him. 'You'd like my help, wouldn't you, Mia?' I gaze at Ricky and a great chasm opens in front of me. I daren't leap. This is my only chance and I'm too afraid to grab it.

'I'd like her to stay, Ricky.'

For a moment, Ricky looks dumbfounded. Then he smiles and nods. Turns away. 'As you like, darling.' He pulls his phone from his trouser pocket. 'Excuse me, it's Sally ringing. I need to have a quiet word with her, there's something I have to tell her. You carry on, Mia. Do as you please. You can decide later if it was worth it.'

CHAPTER 11

Lindy

From the other side of the road, where I sat in my car, Mia's house looked just like all the other houses on the estate. But now I see it's different. I had it all wrong. What a perfect performance she and Ricky put on. So good that even I, her stalker, never saw that the whole thing was a lie.

'I want her to stay.' I was glad she had said that. In any case, I was going nowhere. She looked dreadful. When I found her passed out on the settee, her face white, her hair a mess, I thought she'd had a stroke or something.

When I pulled up outside the house and heard the sound of banging, I couldn't tell at first where the noise was coming from. Then I saw her at the window, hanging onto the curtain. It looked as if someone behind her was dragging her away. I heard her shouting, but I couldn't make out the words, apart from my name.

Convinced an intruder was in there, attacking her, I beat on the front door with my fist, and rang the bell until I thought it might break. Ricky's car stood in the drive, which was unusual. Ricky never walks anywhere apart from when he's playing golf. When nobody opened the door, I ran to the window where I'd seen Mia, but she was gone. The house was silent.

I immediately thought that whoever was in the house must be holding Mia hostage. Then the front door opened and Ricky appeared. He looked surprised.

'What's going on?' I panted. 'Where's Mia? Is she OK?' Behind him, I could hear someone whimpering quietly.

'She's fine, thank you. What's the matter? Why were you banging on the door like that?' The hostility in his look made me step back.

I cleared my throat. 'I saw her at the window. She was banging on the glass, calling my name as if she needed help.' I tried to peer round him, but he stood blocking my view.

Ricky smiled and pushed his hands into his trouser pockets. He was dressed for work, in navy suit trousers and a white shirt that had a dirty brown stain on the front. 'I don't know what you think you have seen, Lindy. It is Lindy, isn't it? We've never been properly introduced.' He put out his hand. I went to shake it, then thought better of it and pushed past him into the house. *Never properly introduced* — bollocks. He knew who I was all right. I was the one who'd irritated the hell out of him at the markets. 'Mia is asleep,' he said. 'She couldn't have been banging on the window. We had the TV on, maybe that's what you heard.' Smug bastard. That might have worked with some ninety-year-old granny with cataracts, but there's nothing wrong with my eyesight. It was such a poor excuse even he was blushing, there was definitely a pink tinge to his cheeks.

'If she's asleep, how come the TV is on so loud I could hear it through your double-glazing?' The pink tinge deepened. Now I was really frightened. What would I find?

I continued on, into the house. You're probably wondering why it didn't cross my mind that he might have done me some harm. There were only the two of them in the house and she was whimpering as if she was in pain. He might have been a serial killer, a psychopath. I suppose you think I'm stupid. Well, that's just the way I am, always the one to blunder in, the idiot who steps in front of the moving bus to save that lame dog from being run over. Small wonder I barged in.

Ricky sighed. 'You'd better come in and see for yourself. She's not been well, and . . . well, when you see her you'll know what I mean.' He trailed after me towards the open door that led into the living room.

'Why didn't you answer the door?' I threw over my shoulder. 'What were you doing in here? How come it took you so long if you were only watching TV?'

Ricky said nothing. The house was silent. I knew Mia had two dogs. I even knew their names — Stan and Ollie. Not a bark. No scrabbling paws as they came running. The house was tidy. Too tidy. 'Where are the dogs?'

'They're staying with Mia's sister, Beth. I didn't know you'd met them.'

I nod. 'Mmm. I met them at one of Mia's coffee mornings. They're devoted to her. Why are they with Beth? Mia hates being parted from them.'

Then I see her, slumped on a small settee over in a little alcove off the room. She didn't look well at all. Ricky followed me over, practically breathing down my neck. 'She looks dreadful. What's the matter with her?' I bent down and shook her gently. 'Mia? Wake up, honey. It's me, Lindy. I heard you calling from the window. Are you Ok? What's wrong with you?'

'She's got herself in a bit of a state, I'm afraid. She's been diagnosed with severe asthma and she may be allergic to the dogs. That's why Beth has them.'

'This is all very sudden,' I say, shocked. 'I didn't know she suffered from asthma.'

'Well, you're not that close, are you?' he said, eyeing me suspiciously. 'I mean, you're only acquaintances. Mia doesn't talk about you much.'

Well, that's true. As far as she's concerned, I'm just the observer. I thought I knew a lot about her, now I know that I only saw what they — or was it he — wanted me to see, not what was really going on.

After we got Mia to her bedroom, I refused to budge. Ricky's sickly-sweet behaviour made me uncomfortable. It didn't ring true. I think I've told you about that gut instinct I have. I watched her while she slept. She looked dehydrated and so thin she was positively gaunt. Ricky told me she lost her appetite when the dogs left.

Waiting for her to wake up, I think that Mia's life isn't that different from mine after all. She has a nicer home, of course, in a quiet suburban estate with a lovely view over the fields. I wonder how long it will be before the pasture land is sold for housing. In the distance, I hear the rattle of a train coming or going from the nearby station. Soon, the same round dog-walker will be coming by. The dog will poop on Mia's lawn just as it always does, and the woman will pick it up with a black poo bag.

Chelford was so charming back in the day, when we first moved here. Friendly faces, a few little shops, a train station handy for going into Manchester when we didn't want to use the car. We often used the train when we went drinking after work. It all seems so long ago now.

At first, we didn't know anyone. They treated us the way people in a small village always do — with suspicion. We soon made friends by using the local shops. When our life flipped over they were all there to support us. Trouble is, I didn't want their help, it felt like interference. All that pity. That kindness. Their sad faces. I pulled away. They thought I was rude. I was.

Now they mostly ignore me. Frank doesn't go out much, and when he does, they avoid him too, because he looks so goddamn scary. 'Hold my hand, children. Let's cross the road to the other side. We'll come back later and buy your sweets when the scary man's gone.' That's the parents. I've heard them. Others avoid eye contact. They whisper, 'Terrible what happened. Lost his mind, you know. I've never seen them out together since it happened.'

* * *

When Mia woke up she didn't want me to leave. That pissed Ricky off. I wouldn't budge, though. I stuck to her like gum on the sole of your shoe. Every excuse Ricky threw at me, I batted away with a smile on my face. By the time I left, I was sure he wanted to kill me. He'd always disliked me anyway.

But there came a point when I had to go, even I couldn't sit in their bedroom forever. And realistically I had no proof, did I? I didn't really know what was going on, what he was doing to her. After all, it was still his house and I had no right to be there if I wasn't wanted.

I left, kissing Mia, whispering to her that I would be back. That's when I noticed the bruises on her wrist.

CHAPTER 12

Mia

Ricky has gone to work without locking me in the pantry. I am creeped out by this sudden change of mood. After all the cruelty, his kindness is disconcerting.

Oh, he hasn't left me to my own devices. I'm not to just chill out and have a nice day. No, before he left for work at 4 a.m., he told me he expected the house to be spotless when he got home, with a meal ready on the table. Apparently, we're to eat together.

When I open the fridge, I'm stunned to find it full of food, including treats, as if it had never been emptied. There's a newspaper on the counter and the TV is on. The radio is back in its usual place. Maybe he realises he won't get away with it, not now Lindy has been here and witnessed the state I'm in. I can't bring myself to believe he's had a change of heart, though it's something to hang on to.

My laptop is back on the kitchen table. I open it and switch it on. It powers up, asking for my password. Ricky told me he'd changed it. I give it a go and I'm in! So he lied about it. Surprised, I sit back in my chair, wondering what is going on. Why would he give me access to the internet and my emails? I look around and sure as dammit, there is my mobile by the landline.

I sit back down with my mobile in my hand and my laptop on. I have all the tools I need to get help, and yet I'm unable to do anything. He said he wanted this evening to be a special one for the two of us. His erratic behaviour is so confusing I'm paralysed, afraid to act.

After Lindy left, he told me my mother wasn't really coming over, but he'd had to get her out of the house somehow. She was interfering, he said. *And challenging*, I thought. He doesn't like that. He sat on the bed and handed me a glass of water, which I refused. He smiled knowingly. 'You don't suspect me of foul play, do you, Mia?' he said, looking hurt. He was so convincing I thought he might actually be sincere. I apologised, which made him smirk. Then I hated myself for being so gullible. He patted my hand. I pulled it away and asked him why he let her back in the house if he despised her so much.

'She's the sort that won't stop badgering.'

Hope washed over me. I truly hoped Lindy wouldn't stop badgering.

Opening my phone, I find tons of messages from both Beth and Lindy. Why hasn't Ricky answered them? What if I ring them and tell them what's been going on? They'll both be over in a shot. And then what? I'd have to tell Beth about Sally and Martin. I'd have to tell Dad that his brother is a rapist. And after that, I'd have to tell Sally. My beautiful Sally. It will destroy her. There has to be another way to escape the hands of my greedy, fucked-up husband.

My mobile rings and I jump. The number is blocked. My finger hesitates above the answer button. What if it's one of my other girlfriends? I can't talk to them; I haven't thought of a story to explain my absence and I don't know what Ricky has said to them. I could make my situation worse. I don't want to anger him. I don't want to go back in the cupboard.

It won't be a friend — their name would be in my contacts. Who then? I answer the call.

'Good morning, darling, how are you today?' Ricky asks. I can tell he's smiling, there's probably someone else in the room and he's acting the concerned husband. What has he told them? Is he weaving an elaborate lie about me so when I do something out of the blue, they'll believe his story?

'What are you up to, Ricky?'

'I don't know what you mean. I hope you've seen all the goodies I've left for you. You've obviously found your phone. Why not call some of your friends? I'm sure that Lindy woman would like to speak with you. She was very concerned about you. Why not ask her over and let her see you're all right?'

I frown. What's his game with Lindy? 'Ricky, we have to sort this out, we can't go on like this.'

'Of course we do. And you know just how to do it, sweetie, don't you? Are you ready to give it a go? I could make the appointment and we can go tomorrow, then the whole thing will be settled.' I wonder who's in the background, who he's playing to.

'No. Stop telling me to do that. You know I won't go through with it.'

'Then we'll have to carry on as before. I thought you'd had enough and having everything back would change your mind.'

'I have my phone. I'll call the police. I'll call Beth and Lindy. Sod the consequences.' In that moment I want to kill the evil fuck. But he knows I won't do any of those things. I can't tell them, or get the police involved without Sally and Dad learning the truth. Ricky knows that. He knows I'll suffer anything to protect them from that knowledge. So what's he playing at?

'Things don't have to be like this, Mia.' He's whispering now. 'It's only money. How can money be more important than your daughter and your father? Which is worth more to you?'

* * *

I'm meeting Lindy. It's just after eleven in the morning. The rain has stopped and there's a gentle breeze. The air is humid, with the prospect of more rain. The park in Knutsford is deserted — who wants to sit on wet swings or slither down a damp slide? I'm grateful for the quiet. I sit on a bench seat, waiting. It's somewhere I can talk and not be overheard. Besides, I couldn't face going into a busy coffee shop or restaurant. It's been ages since I faced people, and I know I don't look great. I do feel a bit better today, though. I've more energy from the food, although he's stopped it again now.

Ricky needs control. I've learned that lesson well over the years. He won't be giving me freedom, not him. He'll have put a tracker on my phone, or my car.

It isn't just now either. I can't believe how long it's taken me to wake up and realise he's been controlling me all our married life. I wonder what he would have done if he had found the letters years ago. What was he looking for inside the old Dansette record player? Mum and Dad bought it for me on my sixteenth birthday, and I've never been able to throw it out. It holds too many memories. It reminds me of lazy Sundays spent sitting around listening to records with my friends and drinking gallons of Coke and Tizer. I thought it was the safest place to hide them, nobody would ever think to look for them there, would they? Well, Ricky did.

Looking back, there was little love between us after we got married. We put on a good show when we were out together, but Ricky was away a lot, building his career. Or so I thought. After the girls arrived, I was glad of the respite. When he wasn't here I didn't have to worry about keeping up appearances. He always liked me made up when he got home. No sweat pants for me, no top with sick dribbled down the front. The house had to be tidy, the children seen but not heard. When he was away, I was relieved to be able to relax and just let go.

I reckoned the sex wasn't great because of what had happened to me with Martin — at least that's what I thought. I was always tense. Sex made me feel ashamed and somehow dirty.

The knowledge that I had lied to him about who Sally's father was made the whole thing worse. I've never been a good liar. Surprising, really, that I've managed to keep this one for over twenty years. Most likely Ricky had affairs. I never even considered the possibility. Maybe I turned a blind eye because I was grateful it kept him away from me.

I've worked out why Ricky has been nice to me today, and has left me all that food. It's the work do he wants me to attend. He'll want me looking good for it, fed and watered like a prize cow.

I haven't used my laptop. He'll have put some spyware on it. I don't trust the camera either. In any case, I have no idea what to search for.

Here's Lindy, strolling towards me. 'Hi! Sorry I'm late. I couldn't find anywhere to park, it's so busy in town.'

'Well, none of them are here, thankfully.' I sweep an arm around the empty park. 'Thanks for coming.' I return her hug and can't help welling up, remembering her concern for me. I must be strong and not break down. I've thought over what I'm going to tell Lindy. I can't keep it bottled up any longer, I need to tell someone. Lindy isn't family, so it'll be easier. She doesn't know my children or my parents. I think I have all the details straight. It's been going on for so long you might think it'd be hard to remember. But remember I do. Every last detail. Everything I felt while it was happening. Every last thought that passed through my mind. I remember my faraway place, the place that kept me sane.

She smells of cooking. She's come straight from work. Her coat is unbuttoned and I can see her uniform. Her blonde hair is coming loose from the hair clip holding it back. She sits next to me, too close. I move away a little. I'm not used to being close to people.

'What's going on, Mia? It's obvious you're in some kind of trouble. Do you want to talk about it? What's going on in that house of yours?'

'Let's walk. I can talk better if we walk. Do you mind?' I'm restless. Lindy shoots straight from the hip like all good

Americans do. No dancing around sensitive issues for Lindy, she's straight in with it. Everyone else I know, even Beth, would test the water first. That's why I chose Lindy to hear my story. Only Lindy can help me.

The rain starts again but we've both brought umbrellas. We continue on around the duck pond. A little girl in a yellow mac, mother in tow, is throwing bread for the ducks.

Lindy pulls a crumpled tissue from her coat pocket and blows her nose. 'I'm off until three, so we have plenty of time. If you're not done by then, I'll just call in sick. You talk, honey. Tell it how you like, I ain't going nowhere.'

I like her accent. I wonder about her, what her life is like. Lindy's a little odd. I get the feeling her blunt tone is hiding something.

I stop for a moment to let a jogger pass. I take a breath. 'Something happened to me a long time ago. I was . . . well, I was raped.'

'No! Who by? Not Ricky?'

I shake my head. I turn away from her searching gaze and think, *those park bins need emptying*. 'I haven't spoken about it to anyone in twenty-five years. Ricky found out about it from some old letters I wrote soon after it happened. He came across them when he was clearing out the loft. And Ricky's having an affair, by the way.'

With an impatient gesture, Lindy dismisses this last statement. 'Who was it? Is he still around? Does Ricky know him? Sorry, Mia — all these questions. How insensitive I sound. It's just that when you said you wanted to talk, that wasn't what I expected.' A beat. 'Has it got something to do with what's going on at home?'

We continue past the pond, up towards the car park where on Sundays I used to bring Sally and Annie sledging when they were little. It's on a slight elevation and pretty safe.

'Yes, it has. He's using it to blackmail me.' I tell her everything. About Martin being Sally's father and my father's brother. If Ricky tells Sally and my Dad, their lives will be destroyed, they'll never recover. Lindy listens in silence.

'Fuck. Listen, Mia. I have to tell you something.' Pulling her coat tighter around her, Lindy says quietly, 'I know about Ricky having an affair. I found out that day I saw you at the markets.'

'Why didn't you tell me?'

Lindy holds up her hand. 'Whoa! Wait a second. Hear me out. I was going to find out more before I said anything, but then it all went mental, what with you quitting your job, and the dogs and all that. And I couldn't get hold of you — the Monday girls' night out was cancelled, and the coffee morning put off.' I look at her oddly. 'I know I've never been invited and I'm not part of your intimate circle of friends. But bar turning up at your house this was the only way I would have got to speak with you.'

'Ok,' I say, feeling hurt.

'Yeah, well, I know who the other woman is.'

'Who is it?' I stop walking.

'Dr Saville from the local practice.'

'Oh my God! She's my doctor! She's Ricky's doctor too. Isn't that unethical? Isn't there a law against that sort of thing?'

'I think it's called malpractice. I'm pretty sure she could be struck off if the health authorities found out.'

'I think he started being really weird with me not long after the affair began. But this . . . cruel behaviour is since he found the letters. He wants to get hold of the money before he leaves me.'

'Mia, is it worth holding out? Why not give it to him? You run the risk of hurting your daughter, your father too. It's only money. Let him have it so he can go. What if he goes too far? What if he gets desperate? You said he spoke about an "accident" happening. What if he tries something?'

'You don't understand.'

'No, I don't. Why is the money so important that you're willing to stake your daughter's life on it? She's worth more than that. I don't know what to say to you, Mia. You're putting yourself through all this for . . . for money?'

'Of course not,' I say. 'It's more complicated than that. You see, my grandmother guessed what happened. She told me Martin had done it before. He'd raped several women. She didn't know if there were any more babies, but she'd paid them off anyway.

'When I told her I was pregnant, she said he'd gone too far. She was ready to cut him off and call the police, but I didn't want that. People would know who my baby's father was, and I didn't want her to live with the stigma. And Martin and my dad were so close. Knowing what Martin was would kill him. So I begged my grandmother to keep quiet.

'Then Ricky came along. To her he was a blessing in disguise. I wasn't in love with him and didn't think I was ready for marriage. Grandma told me I had to get married before I started to show. What man would want to marry me then? Remember, this was twenty-five years ago, things have moved on a lot since those days. She was right, of course. What if Martin guessed that the child was his? He'd want to get involved — or, worse, torment me and Dad.'

'Your dad? I thought you said they were close?'

'They were, but Martin has always envied Dad. He's always saying that everything Dad touches turns to gold, that he's got where he is through pure luck. But Dad's not just lucky, he's smart and savvy and works hard. Martin isn't a worker, and Dad is always having to bail him out. He set him up with the jewellery business and ran it with him so he didn't mess it up, like all his other ventures.'

'But your family's rich, aren't they? Why did he have to start a business at all?'

'My grandfather set up his inheritance in such a way that to receive any of it, his sons had to prove they could make their own way in the world. They didn't have to make loads of money, they just needed to show they could stick at something. The better they did, the more money they received. Martin kept failing. He fell further and further behind my dad.'

'Do you think that's why he raped you? To get back at your dad?' Lindy says.

106

Jesus, the thought had never crossed my mind. Suddenly, I am terribly hot. The heat travels up from my abdomen to the top of my head. My hair is damp with sweat. 'God, sorry. Having a hot flush,' I mutter.

Lindy helps me off with my coat. 'You don't look like you're having one,' she says. 'Me, I go red in the face.'

I am silent, wrestling with the suggestion she's thrown at me.

'Anyway,' she continues, 'whatever Martin's motive was, right now you have to think about Sally. She's your daughter. She needs your protection above all else. You have to give Ricky the money. This is crazy, Mia. Sally is precious. I would die for my girls, I would suffer anything to keep them safe. She's your bloody daughter, Mia. What are you thinking?'

'The thing is, Lindy, my grandfather loved Sally — sadly he only had three years with her before he died. He never liked Ricky, didn't trust him at all. He believed Ricky only wanted me for my money. He never got on with Martin either. He gave me that money as a gift for Sally. He made me promise to keep it safe and that I must keep it in a separate account in her name. But I forgot all about it. Ricky must have been thinking of leaving me, and wanted to sort out our finances when he came across the account.'

'So why not just put it somewhere where he can't get his hands on it? Put it in a trust or something. I'm sure if you spoke to a lawyer, they'd be able to help you. Then he won't be able to do anything about it.'

She's beginning to sound exasperated.

'It's not that easy, Lindy. Ricky has threatened to tell Sally if I try anything like that. And you can't hide an account, the bank will know about it and it will come to light if there's a divorce. Either way, I can't win. I don't trust him not to tell her, even if I do give him the money.'

'But he's her dad! He raised her. He's only just found out about this, it can't change how he feels about her. How can he want to hurt her? What kind of monster is he?'

I shrug. That's the question. 'I don't care if he takes the house and all my money, but he's not having my children's inheritance. Don't you see? He's going to tell them anyway. He'll do it to hurt me. Oh God, I don't know what to do. I have to think of some way to stop him.'

'Suppose you went to the press and told them what he was doing. It would ruin his career. Have you thought of that?'

'Of course I have, I'm not a complete idiot. It comes down to the same thing — Sally's life splattered all over the papers, my family destroyed. And Martin dragged up for raping me. No thank you.'

Lindy is quiet for a long time. I'm just about to say I might as well go home, she says, 'Mia, I think I have an idea. You're not going to like it, but it's the only way out of it that I can see.'

We can't see much anyway. There isn't much light today because of the low-hanging cloud. It's a miserable day altogether. I listen to what she has to say and watch her wait for my response.

'Why would I do that for you?' She's out of her mind. I can't begin to even contemplate what she's suggesting. It's ludicrous. I glance around, but of course there's no one in earshot.

'I'm sorry but I can't talk about it. It hurts too much.'

'But I need to know before I agree.' She must be mad to suggest such a thing. I'm so mixed-up that don't know what to think. 'You can't ask such a thing and not tell me why you want me to do it. It's insane, and besides, we'd never get away with it.'

She grabs my arm and turns me to face her. 'You have to trust me, Mia. You'll understand why when I tell you, I just can't do it right now.'

I study her face. Is she mad? Maybe she's on drugs. Was Ricky right, and she is weird? What she's suggested is messed up. Not to mention one-sided. And against the law.

'I have never told anyone about what happened to me. They said I should see a therapist but I never have. Frank wants us to go together. Well, that won't happen. I can deal with it by myself, in my own way.' She speaks in a monotone, as if she's repeated it over and over, like a lesson she has had to learn.

The silence between us is uncomfortable, thick with things unsaid. I don't know where we can go from here. All the things I've told her. What she's suggested. As if to fill the silence, Lindy says how easy it will be to pull it off. She says she's been waiting a long time to find the right person, and that as soon as she set eyes on me she knew I was the one. She tells me how she stalked me. She knows the number of times my daughters have come to the house. Knows the meals I've served, and my shopping habits. Although she was fooled into thinking that Ricky and I had the perfect marriage. It made her wonder if she'd chosen the wrong accomplice, until she saw him and that woman at the Dahlia.

'I followed any number of women, but none of them seemed just right. They didn't have that little something. I can't tell you how happy I was when I realised I'd got it right with you.'

Suddenly cold, I push her away from me. All the times she bumped into me — at the supermarket, the doctors' surgery. The gym, the pub, the hotel. Was I giving out some subconscious message to her?

'Do you think I'm a terrible person for allowing Martin to do what he did and get away with it?'

'No. I'm sorry if I've given you that impression. It's not how I feel. Listen, Mia. This can only be done the once, and only my way. There's no way out of this for you except with me.'

'But you won't tell me why you want to do it.'

She stares at me. 'No. I can't tell you, but I *will* help you.'

'And I'll help you.'

She nods.

'But you won't tell me why.' I keep pushing but she shakes her head.

'No. You'll just have to trust me. It's for a good reason.'

She's not being fair. I've opened up to her but she won't do the same with me. To my mind that's more than a little one-sided.

'And I'm supposed to help you just like that? Well then, cheers. I have to go.' I look at her one more time, hoping that if I start to walk away it will make her change her mind. It doesn't. Feeling lost and more alone than ever, I turn my back on her.

'Don't leave like this, Mia.'

I stop. 'But what you're suggesting is madness.'

'No, Mia, it's not. You're right for me and I'm right for you. I will help you. Think about it. It will resolve all your problems in one go.'

'If you make one move. If you try to go through with your mad idea, I will—'

'What? It'll be too late for you to do anything by then, because you'll be implicated.'

CHAPTER 13

Lindy

I'm late to work this morning and Jack isn't too pleased about it. His eyebrows bunch together and he's twirling his biro between his fingers, like a majorette in a marching band. He's stressed again, I can tell. Jack's always stressed. I can see him wondering what to say to me — should he shout? Should he swear, or just be plain nasty? I do nothing to help him out. I hang up my coat and pocket my mobile, which will add to his exasperation. We all carry our mobiles with us. He's given up telling us not to.

'I'll have to dock your pay, or you can work some of your lunch time. Since you weren't here, I had to deal with the chambermaids this morning; Joanne is slow, tell her she needs to work faster.' He throws me some keys and stomps off, muttering under his breath in Spanish. 'Don't be late again or I take money off you for sure,' he adds just for the sake of it. He will anyway.

'*Cabrón*', I say under my breath. He turns and stares. I smile brightly and march off in the opposite direction. I know he heard me call him an asshole. He won't say anything though.

I stop at the bottom of the back stairs. There's a small mirror on the wall. It's one of those cheap ones that make you look slightly distorted. I examine my reflection. A bit of makeup would do wonders but it's too much effort. I touch the dark circles beneath my eyes. 'Who are you anyway?' I say to my reflection.

I make straight for the huge walk-in fridge beyond the kitchen, yank open the door and pull out the smoked salmon. Jim, the chef, gives me a sideways glance but says nothing. Everyone steals from Jack. It's because he's such a jerk.

Grabbing a slice of bread, I make smoked salmon sandwiches with cream cheese for Joanne and myself. I ram several slices of the delicious fish into my mouth and put what's left back in the fridge. I make a cafetière of coffee, put the whole lot on a tray and slink up the back stairs to find her. 'You didn't see any of that, did you?' I say to the chef on my way out. He shrugs. The eyes of the huge fish he's deboning seem to follow me out of the kitchen.

I tell Joanne to join me in one of the bedrooms. It has peach velour chairs and a chintz dressing table. 'Come on, let's have brunch. Jack's treat.' I set the tray on the dressing table, pull two chairs close to the table and plonk myself down.

'Really? Jack gave us brunch? Wow.' She grabs a sandwich and gives it a sniff. 'God, I'm knackered. He's so bloody picky. Mmm. I don't think I've ever had smoked salmon before. Isn't it expensive?' She puts her feet up on the edge of the dressing table.

I shrug. 'He's such a wanker. He just threatened to dock my wages again, and he wants me to work in my lunch break because I was late in. He forgets I always work longer than my shift anyway, with no extra pay. Idiot.' I lean back in my chair, sandwich in hand, and enjoy the moment.

'What if he catches us?' Joanne peeks under the bread, apparently unsure whether to eat it or not.

'He won't. He'll be having his late morning siesta in his office. We have half an hour.'

'I did the bathrooms in rooms four and five and then he asked me to do them again,' Joanne complains.

The bathrooms are the worst to do. All the chambermaids hate doing them. People are so gross when they stay in hotels. They seem to forget how their bodily functions work. 'Just tell him you've done them, he won't know.'

'I've applied for a job at Aldi,' Joanne says. 'They're recruiting at the moment. I hate their uniform, don't you? But I guess anything is better than working with Jack. You know what he gave us for lunch yesterday? Only the crap the chef was throwing out. The fish smelt rank but he, as usual, insisted it was fine. "This is all you're getting. This or nothing. The people on the streets wouldn't be so fussy." The man should be reported.'

I nod absently. I have a lot on my mind. One day somebody will report him but it won't be me, and clearly not Joanne either.

'Still thinking of driving around the States with your boyfriend, are you?' I envy her being able to take off like that. The open road, nobody to keep a check on you. No clocks. No timetable. Just freedom. After I finished university, I travelled the east coast all the way up to the Canadian border with my then boyfriend, Jackson Dale. I'd known him for ever. We'd been to kindergarten, then school, and we both ended up at the same university. His mother and mine were good friends. We were for ever staying over at each other's houses. I think our parents wanted us to get it together. We're still friends, well, maybe not now. I don't keep in touch with anyone. He's emailed a few times for a catch up, and when *it* happened, he even threatened to come over. I had to be really rude to stop him coming. Jackson Dale's kindness would have been too painful to bear. I don't deserve anyone's kindness. I know I hurt him but he respected my wishes, and I'm grateful to him for that. I don't know what would have happened if he had turned up. He would have killed Frank for a start.

Jackson was very different to Frank. For starters, he was white. He was slimmer than Frank, and shorter. Real Southern charm that boy had. He was a real gentleman. I always felt safe around Jackson Dale. His pale blue eyes would hypnotise you if you weren't careful. He tanned so well, turned a golden colour which made his eyes even bluer, if that was at all possible. All the girls fell for him. He had a gravelly voice, a bit like Rod Stewart. Twin that with his Southern drawl and you had one hell of a sexy guy.

We realised it wasn't going anywhere for us and decided to just stay friends. There wasn't any real chemistry, you see, just a liking. God knows we tried, but it just wasn't there. The memory of the times with Jack make me realise how lonely I am right now. *Well, you deserve it*, I say to myself. I pick at my sandwich, thinking this isn't the life I'd wanted.

I notice Joanne looking at me. I wonder what she would say if I told her my plan. I've been toying with the idea for a long time now, going over the could-I-should-I-will-I until my head hurts. I conclude that even if I told someone, they would never understand. How could they? Nobody knows what I am going through. I finish my sandwich. The half hour is up.

I hear Jack somewhere along the corridor, talking to one of the others. 'Let's shove this lot under the bed till he goes back downstairs,' I tell Joanne. We put the furniture back in place and hurry out.

Downstairs, I'm counting the latest delivery of linen from our laundry when I hear Jack talking to someone. His voice is familiar, it makes the hairs on my neck and arms prickle.

I can't hear any of what Ricky is saying to Jack, apart from my name. Jack is rattling on in his broken English, with the occasional break, which means he's stroking his moustache. I'm about to dart out through the kitchen when Jack turns and points at me.

What's Ricky doing here? What does he want? Surely Mia hasn't told him what I had in mind? That would be crazy, right? She'd said she wasn't interested but I could tell she was. Agreeing to such an outlandish scheme is probably a step too far for Mia right now. She'll get there, although I'm probably going to have to force her hand. Sometimes all people need is a gentle nudge in the right direction. Right now, she's still feeling sorry for herself, she had been hoping I had a simple solution to her problem. Well, I did, only it wasn't one she wanted to hear.

There's no simple solution to the mess she's in, and she knows it. He'll tell Sally even if he does get the money. We have to act quickly, before people see us together and start making connections.

Ricky comes through the kitchen and stands in front of me. Trying to intimidate me, is he? Is that his game? What does he possibly think he can do to hurt me? Nothing. He has no idea what Mia and I have planned for him. I have one over on him already — I know he has a mistress. If you can call it that. His bit on the side. His crumpet.

There's a smirk on his lips that I return with one of my own. *Would you like a room, Dicky Ricky? Is the good doctor coming to give you a thorough going over?* Cheating bastard. He deserves what's coming his way.

In a voice that's pure Scarlett O'Hara, I say, 'Why, Mr Hicks. Is there something wrong?'

'Why would you think that, Lindy?' he says.

'Why else would you come here to see me?'

He forces a laugh. 'I wanted to thank you for spending time with Mia. She's not well and she's been having some, er, *episodes*. I just came to say how much we appreciate your help.'

Bollocks. He's up to something. Look at him, all cool and collected. I guess he learned that through being on TV.

'Episodes? What sort of episodes, Mr Hicks? Panic attacks? Fear of small, enclosed spaces?' That prompts a reaction. I see a little chink in his glossy armour.

'Anyway,' he says dismissively, with a flick of his hand. I've noticed him doing that on the TV. I wonder if it's a nervous twitch, like the way his skin gets pink. 'Thank you again. Perhaps you'll be able to pay Mia another visit soon.'

'Sure.' I wait for him to turn to leave and add, 'Don't worry, I'll be over to see her very soon.' He's halfway down the front steps when I say, 'By the way, has Dr Saville been to the house?'

He stops, one foot in the air. 'Dr Saville? What for?'

'To see Mia, of course. Why else?' He turns and stares at me for a moment, his eyes narrowed. I wave cheerily and go back to the laundry.

* * *

Later, when I finish my shift, I go home, make a flask of coffee, grab a packet of biscuits and head out to the park.

'Where are you going, Lindy?' Frank trails after me out of the house. He looks a mess — baggy jeans, a sweater that's all misshapen and that bloody spaniel look in his eyes.

'None of your business.' I need to be alone.

'Lindy!'

Annoyed, I stop at my car and turn around. 'WHAT?'

'Have you forgotten what today is? I've tried calling you . . .'

My legs give way. Arms outstretched, Frank rushes over to me. No, I hadn't forgotten. I'd just pushed it to the back of my mind. Why the hell did he have to remind me?

I hold up my hands to stop him coming any closer. 'Don't. Don't you dare touch me. Don't come near me.' He keeps coming. 'I swear, Frank, if you come any closer, I will hit you with this flask.' Ignoring the threat, he catches hold of the hand holding the flask and takes it away. I push him. I can't bear him near me. His touch makes me feel dirty. Ashamed. Guilty. I slap him across his face so hard my hand stings. I've never hit anyone before.

Now he's crying. 'Please, Lindy. Please. I'm sorry. I'm so sorry. Please talk to me. We can't go on like this. We need to talk about it. We need to forgive each other.'

'Forgive? Oh, no. You don't get to say that. You don't get forgiveness. You should have listened to me that night. You should have listened.' These last words come out in a scream.

I wrench open the car door, snatch my flask from his grasp and throw it onto the passenger seat along with my handbag and the biscuits. There are some things that are too painful to remember. My hand is shaking so much I can't put the key in the ignition. It takes me three attempts to manage it. I slam the door. Put the car in gear and drive away, leaving Frank on his knees in the driveway, sobbing his heart out.

CHAPTER 14

Mia

I'm in a bit of a state. To be honest I'm wondering if I've misinterpreted what Lindy was trying to say. I must have imagined the whole idiotic idea.

When Ricky comes home, I try to act as usual. There's something up with him, too, because he greets me with a smile. He takes off his raincoat and slings it over the back of a chair before turning to face me. There's an edge to his voice when he asks me how my day has been.

Averting my eyes, I say, 'Oh, fine.'

'So, what were you doing at the park? Meet anyone?'

There's no point lying, so I tell him.

'So, what did you talk about with friend Lindy?' How does he even know I met anyone? 'Concerned for you, is she? What did she say? Call the police? Leave your husband?' He snorts.

Suppose I tell him. Suppose I say, "*As it happens, Ricky, darling, she said I should kill my husband — or rather she will. And I will kill hers. Neat, eh? If we do it like that, there'll be no evidence, you see. Remember that movie, Strangers on a Train? You liked that movie,*

118

didn't you?" Instead, I say she's been worried about me, that's all. She wanted to make sure I was all right.

He steps forward, until we're almost touching. I have to steel myself not to back away. I had been feeling a little more confident after my talk with Lindy, but it's fast ebbing away.

Without warning, he raises his hand and slaps my face. I stare at him, touching my cheek, and he punches me in the belly. I stagger back against the wall and my knees buckle. He smiles cruelly, and runs a finger over the side of my face where he hit me. I flinch at the touch. His eyes on mine, he strokes my neck, my collarbone. I hardly dare breathe. My heart is pounding so loud he must be able to hear.

'I'm taking your bank cards away,' he says, watching for my reaction. 'I've deleted your banking apps from your phone and changed your passwords, so even if you upload them again you won't be able to get in. You won't be needing any money. As for your car, you won't be needing that either. Can't have you taking any more trips, can we?'

He knows I won't run. He's playing with me, seeing how far he can go before he breaks me. All the while his fingers are running over my throat. Suddenly, they close. I can't breathe.

'You won't kill me, Ricky. You won't, I know it.'

'Oh really? You can't know that for sure, can you?'

Involuntarily, I glance at the open pantry door.

'What's up, Mia? Don't you want to go back in there?' His grip on my throat tightens. I am really fighting for breath now. He won't kill me. I hold onto that thought, returning his stare until, finally, I can no longer breathe and stars dance in front of my eyes. In a final effort to break free, I rake my nails over the back of his hands.

He lets me go, and I slide down the wall, gasping for breath. He picks me up and throws me in the pantry. I land on my knees and look up at him. I was wrong. He will kill me if I don't do as he says.

Locked in the dark, I have time to contemplate what Lindy said. My only way out of this is to agree to her plan.

Ricky lets me out the following morning. He hands me a cup of tea. 'There you are. Drink that and smarten yourself up. I hope a night in there has made you think, Mia. I'm assuming you've told Lindy about what's going on. Fine. I don't think she or anyone else is going to believe you.'

I drink my tea, watching him from over the rim of my cup. It hurts to swallow. My feet have pins and needles and I've wet myself too. Not only am I in pain but I'm humiliated as well.

It's funny, isn't it, how easily you can cross a line. It doesn't take much, does it — just a night in the dark — to make you change your mind about what's right and what's wrong. You have to put yourself in someone's shoes before you can judge them. I judged Lindy, although I don't know anything about her. She wouldn't tell me why she wants to do this, but does it really matter? A few simple words from her have transformed me from victim to survivor. It's enough. I don't need to know her reasons.

But what if I was to beg Ricky not to tell? What if I gave him the money? Would he agree? And if he did, could I trust him? I could threaten him. 'If you ever breathe so much as a word to Sally, I will tell the papers about your affair. Your career would be in tatters.' Weak. And, anyway, the damage would already have been done.

What choice do I have? Maybe granny was wrong to make me keep it a secret. Secrets have a way of coming out. So many mights, so many shoulds.

At the root of it all is Martin. He is to blame for where I am now. Martin, the loser. Everything was handed to him on a plate, and he still turned it into a crock of shit.

The more I think about Lindy's idea, the more I think it's my only way out.

'Have you bought yourself something to wear at the awards dinner?' Ricky asks.

'No, I didn't think you'd want me to go with you after what happened yesterday.' To be honest, I thought he'd go with *her*. It's certainly the last thing I want to do.

'I'll take you to Selfridges and we'll choose a dress together. It's good you've lost weight, you'll look better in something clingy.' He eyes me speculatively. 'You need to eat more, though. You're starting to look gaunt. It doesn't suit you. You're hardly the model type, are you?'

So here we are in Selfridges, waiting for the assistant to bring a selection of evening dresses. Ricky has made sure they know who he is and has insisted that we need privacy, in case he is recognised. No one must see my dress until the night. Who does he think he is — some Hollywood star lined up for best actor at the Oscars?

He chooses a long, emerald green silky dress with spaghetti straps and a plunging neckline. I have no say in the matter. To go with it, he buys a huge imitation emerald and diamond necklace, along with shoes with heels so high I can't walk in them. He makes an appointment with my hairdressers.

'You'll have to eat small portions for the next few days. We don't want you getting a belly, do we? Get some colour back in your face too. I'm not having you showing me up, Mia. There'll be competition, you know how it is. I want my wife to look stunning. Not haggard. And you can get rid of that miserable expression. I want smiles. I want affection. I'm hoping to impress, and the image of a happily married couple goes a long way. The press will be there, lapping it up, so you'd better play your part. You wouldn't want me letting anything slip, would you?'

'As if you would. And spoil your reputation? I don't think so.' Then my tongue runs away with me. 'But I can. I can let it slip that you're shagging someone else and your carefully laid plans will all come tumbling down.' Oh, Jesus. Why did I have to say that? Stupid. Stupid.

He grips my arm. He won't make a scene here, though. Not in public. 'You're starting to get wrinkles,' he says. 'Have you noticed? You won't say a thing,' he hisses. 'Little Miss Perfect. Think about it. You might just trip in your new high heels and fall to your death. There's only one loser here, Mia, and it's not going to be me.'

That dress does reach the floor, and those ridiculous heels . . . Is he really thinking of pushing me down the stairs? Maybe it's being out of the house that makes me plunge on. 'Or I could poison you, cut your throat while you're asleep and claim amnesia brought on by your abuse.'

He stares at me. He can't believe I've said that. He'll come at me now, for sure. He struggles with himself for a moment, and glances at the shop assistant who is some way off, arranging dresses on a rail. He smiles. Strokes my face. Gently, he removes the scarf I have draped around my neck to hide the bruises. He touches them.

'Ooh, nasty. We'll have to do something about these. Why don't you go to the spa with your sister?' He's winding me up. He won't let me go. 'How about it, Mia? Fancy a day at the spa?' I see the assistant watching us. She smiles and we both smile back. 'It will be good for your complexion. I'll drive you there and pick you up afterwards.'

Maybe he's so desperate to have me looking good on the night that he means it, he'll let me go to the spa. No, he won't trust me not to spill the beans to Beth.

The assistant wanders away out of sight.

Meanwhile, Ricky is busy on his phone.

Holding his phone up, he turns to me. 'Go to the spa. Tell whoever you like. Nobody will believe you. You see I've just recorded you saying you want to kill me.'

I listen to my damning words. Listen — and decide.

* * *

The following day, Ricky drops me off at Mottram Hall for my day at the spa. He comes inside and checks me in. I guess he wants to make sure I'm not planning to run off somewhere. Let him. I'm out, and I'm seeing Beth. I can hardly wait. It's just so wonderful to be out of the house and away from that pantry.

I can't quite believe I'm here. I've been expecting him to cancel at the very last moment. Before he says goodbye, he bends down and kisses me on the lips. It takes all my strength not to cringe.

'Make sure you have the full works, darling. I want you looking relaxed and glowing.'

The place is decorated in natural earthy colours. Soothing music plays in the background and there is the sound of trickling water. Scented candles are dotted around, sending the fragrance of lavender and sandalwood wafting through the air.

Beth is already here and changed into her fluffy white robe. I leave my clothes in the locker, don my own robe and join Beth.

'How are you, Mia?' Beth asks. We are both on our bellies, waiting for the masseuse. 'I couldn't believe it when Ricky sent me the invitation. What's come over him? He's been so protective of you since this asthma thing. I was sure he'd cancel at the last minute.'

I shrug.

'Look, they're bringing champagne,' she says, 'so we'll have a totally relaxing afternoon. If Ricky's picking you up, you needn't worry about driving. Drink up, Sis, and enjoy.'

'Aren't you driving?' I see they've brought us a whole bottle of champagne.

'I came in a taxi. Ricky can drop me off on your way home. He won't mind, will he?'

Beth's words come out in little gusts each time the masseuse applies pressure to her back.

Suddenly, I'm reminded of my dogs. God, I miss them.

'How are they?' I ask Beth.

'Who?'

'Stan and Ollie, of course. Ricky said he'd been over to see them and they were happy. I'd like to visit them as soon as I can. I can't bear being away from them.'

'Mia, Ricky picked them up two days ago. He said your asthma wasn't great and you'd decided to re-home them. I told him I'd like to keep them but he said you thought it would be too distressing to see them when you came to visit.

I said I'd rather hear it from you, but he insisted on taking them. Come on, Mia. I texted you and you replied that you didn't want to talk about it. You said it was for the best, that it was too painful to even think about, and I should drop it.'

I picture their little faces looking hopefully at Ricky, thinking he was bringing them home. The bastard.

After the massage, we change and head for the restaurant. While Beth is getting dressed, I call Ricky and demand to know where the dogs are.

'I wanted to show you how easily I can take away your loved ones. A few simple texts, and you're left broken. And there's nothing you can do.'

'Where have you taken them? Please, Ricky, at least tell me they're safe.' So this was why he was so keen for me to come to the spa with Beth. He wanted me to find out about my dogs.

'I imagine someone will find them. Maybe. If they're lucky.'

'What do you mean? Where are they?' My voice cracks.

'You really want to know?'

'Just tell me,' I whisper, tears running down my face.

He sighs. 'OK, if I must. I left them tied up somewhere, you don't have to know where. Now perhaps you'll understand how far I'm prepared to go. I want that money, Mia. This time it's the dogs. Next time it'll be your family. Don't cry, Mia. You know what to do.'

In the restaurant, much to Beth's surprise, I order steak and chips. 'You mean you're going to eat all that?' she says. 'Since when do you eat chips?'

'Since . . .' Should I tell her? I weigh up the consequences. 'Since when?'

'Has Ricky said anything to you?' I blow my nose. I will not cry, I won't.

I shove a chip in my mouth, watching her toy with her quinoa. I know Beth better than anyone. When we were small, we argued a lot, as sisters do, but for the most part we got on.

We've always been there for each other, no matter what. She'll go crazy if I tell her about Martin.

'He came over to the house after he took them. He said he wanted to reassure me that they're doing fine. He seemed to have something on his mind.'

I imagine him telling her that I'm really ill. That he's really worried about me. That it's not the menopause making me forget but something much, much worse. Telling her about how I took too many sleeping pills and how lucky it was that he was there to bring me round. He'd tell her how concerned Lindy was when she came to see me, how I stood at the window shouting for help when all he was doing was trying to calm me down.

She stares at me and I'm forced to meet her gaze. 'Mia, what the fuck is going on in that house of yours?'

Relief. She did say that, right? She knows something is going on. I could kiss her. 'Oh, Beth! Thank God you don't believe what he told you.'

'How do you know what he told me?'

'I can guess. He told you I'm unstable and a danger to myself. That he's really worried and that he's looking after me the best he can. I expect he told you Lindy found me unconscious after I'd taken an overdose of sleeping pills.' She puts her knife and fork down with a clatter. 'No, carry on as normal, please. I think he might be watching us.' This brings a look to her eyes. 'Ha, he told you I was paranoid and would probably say something like that, didn't he?'

'Yes, he did. Pretty much the same as you just said. Mia, I believe what you're saying, but you have to tell me what's going on, or how can I help? You look awful, you're far too thin, you had no weight to lose and now look at you.'

'He lied to you, Beth. Shit. Stan and Ollie haven't gone to a good home, he's left them tied up somewhere, abandoned, and they'll die. He won't tell me where they are. How can I find them?' I bite my bottom lip. 'God, say something, Beth, please.' I have to stop myself from screaming.

Beth frowns. 'What are you talking about? He's taken them to that shelter over in High Legh, "Dogs for Life". At least that's what he said.'

'I called him while you were getting changed. He hasn't, Beth, he's lied to you. He's dumped them.'

'But why? What's going on, Mia? Tell me, or I'm going to the police, or . . . or I'll confront him. What's the fucker up to?'

I can barely speak. While I weigh up what to tell her, I'm thinking of Lindy's plan, and if by telling Beth I'll mess it all up. Then there'll be no way out for me. The whole point of Lindy and I doing this is so nobody puts us together. I can't tell her.

'I'm sorry, Beth. I can't tell you.'

My mind is made up. I'll get my revenge. But, first, I have to get my dogs back.

CHAPTER 15

Lindy

I'm walking along King Street when I spot Ricky's car outside one of the restaurants. The doctor stands next to it, lips in a pout, applying lipstick. I stop by a shop a few doors down and watch her. She must be a good few years younger than Ricky. Ricky comes out of the restaurant, they get into the car and drive off, laughing.

They won't be going to his house, so they must be going to hers. I dial the surgery and ask to speak with her.

'Sorry, Doctor Saville has finished for the day. Would you like to speak to one of the other doctors?'

'No, I need to speak to her. I'm calling from Ravenscroft landscaping. She'd ordered two tons of topsoil which is supposed to be delivered today, only the person who took her address has gone on holiday and we can't read her writing. So, if you'd just give me her address . . .'

'I'm sorry but we can't give out personal information.'

'We've tried her mobile but it keeps going to voicemail. If we can't get the delivery out today, it'll have to be next week. I know she's organised the landscapers to start tomorrow.

Could you try and get in touch with her for me?' I know I'm quite safe. The doctor won't answer her phone because she'll be too busy shagging.

'Let me just check with the practice nurse.' The line goes quiet. A few minutes later I'm speaking to a plummy-voiced woman who asks a million questions which I field quite aptly. Before I give up and put the phone down, I give it one last try.

'OK. If you'd just give me your name, I shall inform Dr Saville that we were unable to deliver her load because you refused to give us the address.' I chuckle. 'I'm not sure how well that one'll go down. She insisted it had to be delivered today because the contractors had slotted her in specially. She was a bit scratchy about it to be honest, and I'm not looking forward to being on the receiving end when she finds we haven't turned up with it.'

'Oh, I see. Well, let me try her mobile for you.' She's gone for a few moments. 'I can't get through to her. It's against company policy, but I'll make an exception in this case. The address is twenty-three, Applegate Crescent, Lower Peover. And your name, please?'

My mind goes blank for a second. 'Er, Sarah Smith.'

I drive to Lower Peover. I'm in luck. After several wrong turns — my car is too old for a satnav, and I don't have a fancy phone — I find the road. Ricky's car is parked on her drive. I come to a halt outside a heavily extended bungalow, and get out, just as it starts raining. Another piece of luck, since I can use my umbrella as a shield. I walk back and forth past the house, looking in discreetly in case they're in one of the front rooms. They're not, so I edge past Ricky's car and skirt around the house, thankful that the good doctor has chosen to live in a bungalow.

Music is coming from one of the bedrooms at the back. I peer in. They're on the bed, fucking, going at it like a couple of wild animals. I'm impressed; she hadn't struck me as the athletic type. I'm sure I've never been that energetic, even when I was her age. Their clothes are scattered all over the floor, and Dr Saville is wearing nothing but a black lacy bra.

I have an idea. I tiptoe over to the back door, being careful not to knock over the plant pots. I'm not expecting it to be open, but I give it a go. It's unlocked. I take a step inside and look around. God, what an untidy woman. I'll think twice before going to see her for any ailment, I might catch something. There are plates on the table with the encrusted remains of food on them that must have been there for days.

I can hear their moans coming from the bedroom. It's not an attractive sound. Now they're giggling like a pair of naughty children. I'm sure I hear Mia's name. So, I think, they're both in this together. Doctors are supposed to help people. The only person this doctor is helping is herself.

Suddenly I realise they have fallen silent, and get out, quick. I think of Mia.

CHAPTER 16

Mia

Ricky doesn't pick me up. I try to call him, but I can't get through. I leave messages on his voicemail. Nothing. In the end, I call a taxi. Beth insists on coming home with me. She can see how worried I am. Now that she knows about Stan and Ollie, she's raging.

When we arrive at the house, his car is on the drive. Confused, Beth asks the taxi driver to wait while she comes inside with me. I feel a bit light-headed — too much champagne and too little food. I lost my appetite after learning about the dogs.

On our way home in the taxi, I made Beth promise not to confront Ricky about Stan and Ollie. Being Beth, she doesn't listen. As soon as we're in the door, she demands to know where the dogs are. 'You told me you'd taken them to "Dogs for Life". Now Mia tells me you've abandoned them somewhere. Tell me where they are, this minute, you sick, twisted bastard. I'm going for them, right now.'

Afraid to face him, I go straight upstairs to the bedroom. I can hear them arguing. I can't bear to think about my dogs, it hurts too much. They'll be so scared. Beth is trying to help me, but shouting at Ricky is not the way to go about it. He already looked angry when we arrived. Maybe he'll tell her where they are just to shut her up. Yeah, and maybe pigs will fly.

I lock my bedroom door and lean against it. I need to take control here. I'll change into my jeans and go with Beth. I can't bear another moment knowing they're out there, and what might have happened to them. I've always thought that anyone capable of hurting an animal has a dark, evil soul. If nothing else, this has focused my mind and made me even more determined to act.

I want to call Lindy, and tell her I'll do whatever she wants. I just need him out of my life.

He has set up my phone so that he can read my text messages. The landline is no use; he just needs to re-dial the last number and he'll know who I've called. I need to get hold of her. Beth is going to antagonise him and he'll take it out on me. He can do what he likes, so long as it brings Stan and Ollie back home. He won't hurt me tonight, though. I have to look my best for his special awards event tomorrow. Perhaps I can borrow someone's phone when I'm there. I find her number in my contacts and memorise it.

I go to my wardrobe intending to pull out the new dress and hang it on the front of the door. It's gone. Everything is gone. My wardrobe is empty. I open my chest of drawers. Empty. I look around me. There is nothing in my room. All my drawers have been cleared. The dressing table has nothing but the mirror and a stick of red lipstick. My things have gone from the bathroom.

I open my bedroom door, about to go and ask him what is going on. Ricky is standing outside, his arms folded across his chest, staring at me, his eyes blazing. He looks as if he might kill me at this very moment.

'Where's Beth?' I ask, knowing full well she's gone.

'Oh, Beth.' He shrugs. 'Maybe I've put her with Stan and Ollie.'

'Come on, she's only just got here. Where is she?' Has he hurt her? Needing to check she's OK, I take a step forward.

He puts a hand on my shoulder and pushes me back roughly. 'Wouldn't you like to know. Maybe she's tied up in the garage. Or in the pantry. Best place for that bitch.' He shoves me again. I stumble back.

He looks angry, angrier than I've ever seen him before. Now I'm truly terrified.

'Just like you. Two bitches. You've really gone too far this time, Mia.'

'What are you talking about?'

'Don't play the innocent with me. Did you think I wouldn't know it was you? Turn you on, did it, watching us? Is that why you followed me? Is it? Maybe you wanted to join in.' I have no idea what he's talking about. 'Well, I'll tell you this, she's a better shag than you'll ever be. Boring Mia, who never gets excited. You like to watch, though, don't you?'

He moves towards me, and I back away. He's ranting, not making sense. I cast around for something to use as a weapon. But there's nothing here. From the other side of the bed, where I've retreated, I say quietly, 'Ricky, why didn't you pick me up? Where were you?'

He flies at me then, throwing me backwards. He grabs me by my hair and pushes me until I'm pinned against the wall. 'You know damned well where I was, you dirty little voyeur.'

'Ricky, I've been at the spa where you left me. Let go of me, you're hurting. Ricky, stop it. I don't understand what you're saying.'

He mimics my voice. 'Stop it, Ricky. You're hurting me, Ricky. Ricky. Ricky. Ricky.'

He slaps me on the face. 'Ricky, don't. What am I supposed to have done?'

He pushes me down on the bed and rips off my clothes. 'Is this what you want? You want me to fuck you like I fucked Christine?'

'Who's Christine?' By now I'm so confused I don't connect the name with Dr Saville. I hear the sound of a zipper. He's taking off his trousers, while keeping me pinned to the bed. I wriggle and twist beneath him. He's never done this before. Was it Beth, interrogating him about the dogs? Or was it the spa? Did he let me go just so he could punish me for it later? What did he mean by *voyeur*? In the midst of my panic and bewilderment, it dawns on me who Christine must be — Dr Saville. 'Ricky. I am telling you the truth. I've no idea what you think I've done, but you've got it wrong.'

'Bitch. I've had enough of your pig-headedness. The day after tomorrow you will go to the fucking bank with me and put my name on that account. I've already told Sally to come home because I have something important to tell her. After that, I'll be seeing darling Daddy. Today's stunt was the last straw.'

With that, he enters me, so hard I scream out in pain. With each brutal thrust, he says, teeth gritted, 'You came to her house. You saw us fucking. Well, you will pay for that with more than money.'

When he's done, he rolls off me, breathing hard. I can smell his sweat.

Crying, shaking so much my teeth chatter, I think of Lindy. Oh, God, Lindy. She knew about Christine Saville. It must have been her who followed him.

'And another thing,' he says from the door. 'You will stay in here until we go to the bank. I'll be going to the awards dinner on my own because my poor darling wife is sick. I've disconnected the landline and your mobile is with me. If anyone tries to contact you, I will respond. And don't get any smart ideas about escaping. Nothing is going to stop me telling them, nothing. Unless you kill me, but you're too feeble and pathetic for that.' He closes the bedroom door. I hear the key turn in the lock.

Curled up under the duvet, sore and aching, I give way to tears. There's no way out now.

I imagine Ricky sitting Sally down, all fatherly, and dropping the bombshell. I see myself watching from the doorway, grubby and ashamed and unable to move. My beautiful daughter's face will be crumpled in pain. She'll push me away if I go to her. She'll hate me. And what about Annie? How will she feel?

What if I had told Dad about what happened? Would he and Mum have made me have an abortion? Probably. I might well have agreed. Then my lovely daughter would never have been born.

Things happen for a reason. *That* happened so Sally could live. I wouldn't change that for anything in the world. Out of nothing but greed, Ricky is willing to destroy the lives of two wonderful people. Anger gives me strength, and I stop crying. He will not destroy my daughter's life. I need to get in touch with Lindy. We have only two days to carry out her plan.

Sometime later, I hear Ricky leave. I rush to the bedroom window just in time to see him pull out of the drive. I need to get out of this room. I shake the door, rattle the handle. It doesn't budge.

I take a shower to get the smell of him off me. He hasn't even left me a towel. I dry myself with the duvet. There's a pair of joggers and a black jumper in the laundry basket. Now to get hold of Lindy.

I go to the door and squint through the keyhole. He's left the key in the lock. If I can knock it out, I might be able to pull it back under the door. I kneel down and push my fingers under the door. I can just about get them through as far as my knuckles. If only I had a piece of paper. Of course, there's not a single scrap in the room. Still, I might be able to reach that key.

I kick the door just under the lock. Then again, harder. Then harder still. After six tries, I think I might have damaged my foot.

Frustrated, I sit on the floor, pull my knees back to my chest and with all my strength, launch both feet at the door.

The door shakes, the jolt sends an agonising pain up to my hip. I kneel down and peer under the door. There, lying on the landing carpet, is the key. Now all I need to do is get hold of it. *Think, Mia, think.* I feel under the door but it's just out of reach.

Then it occurs to me that there's a small window in the bathroom above the toilet. Maybe, just maybe, Ricky forgot to lock it. I'm so skinny now I might be able to squeeze through. The garage roof is below it, it's flat and not too big a drop.

Climbing onto the toilet lid and opening the window, I work out that the best way to do it is head first. I twist around and push my arms through, then haul and wriggle my way out. My shoulders catch for a moment but after more twisting I am through. The problem is I am head down. I'll knock myself out if I fall forward on the hard surface, so I get back inside. I hurry to the bedroom, grab the duvet and pillows and throw them out. Now I have a soft landing, I wriggle back out and drop onto the roof.

Ricky has set up a camera in the bedroom. He can't watch it while he's driving, which gives me about half an hour to get hold of Lindy. I glance at my watch. He'll be in Manchester in about five minutes.

The garage roof isn't that high, and I land on the grass anyway. We keep the remote hidden in a plant pot. I go in and make my way through to the kitchen.

My phone is lying near the cooker. Thank God. He can pick up any messages for me on his phone. If I use it, he'll see. The landline is unplugged but still on the windowsill.

I plug the landline back into the wall and dial Lindy. No answer. Where is she?

Massaging my sore hip, I go through the call log on my phone. Beth and Lindy have both called. I wonder what he told them. There are no texts, no voice messages.

I pull off the tea towel that is draped over the oven door. I drag one of the kitchen chairs over to the camera in the corner and stand on it. I throw the tea towel over the camera. I glance at my watch. Any minute now he'll be checking his phone.

Limping a little, I drag the chair and another tea towel out into the hallway and cover this camera too. I feel better knowing he can't see me. I limp back to the phone and call Lindy again. It rings and rings. I contemplate calling Beth, but I need to keep her out of this. I also need a reliable alibi. From directory enquires I get the number for the Dahlia hotel. In my panic, I'd forgotten she'd be at work.

'Lindy, I need to speak to you . . . Yes, I'll do it. But I need to get out of this house right away. I can't stay here any longer . . . No, he's lost the plot. I'm scared he might kill me. He's given me till after the awards thing, then he's taking me to the bank. He's called Sally and asked her to come and see us. He's going to tell her and my dad. He thinks I was spying on him with that woman. I guess it was you, but he thinks it was me. We have to do it now . . . What? No, I'm not hysterical, just bloody terrified . . . What? I don't care whether you tell me or not . . . Right now, Lindy. I can't see another way out of this. And I want to tell Beth . . . I know, I know. But I've told her what Ricky's been doing, she knows what's going on here . . . Sorry, but she's my sister. Another thing, he's dumped my dogs and I have to find them first. I don't know where . . . What? No, of course he's not here. He's gone to the awards do in Manchester . . . Drinking? I guess so . . . No, he won't drive back, he'll probably get a taxi, or maybe stay at her house . . . Why? Why do you need the spare car key? . . . Really? Oh my God. Why didn't I think of that? I'm coming with you. I'll see you there.'

CHAPTER 17

Lindy

I tell Jack I'm not feeling well and need to go home. He tells me to take some paracetamol. I tell him it's tummy trouble, scrunching up my nose so he works it out.

'I hope you not give it to no one.' He rolls his eyes. 'Remember, Lindy, I not give you sick pay. You no work, I no pay.' Walking away, he wipes his hands on his trousers as if he's afraid of catching the bug. Just to annoy him, I cough in his direction. Scowling, he speeds away. Jerk. I head out into the rain.

I kind of have a plan in my head. You know the sort. The kind that's a bit like a jigsaw that you piece together over time. You move the pieces around in your head, to see which one fits where. Then you have the picture.

Now, though, I'm not so sure. I read a book recently. Wanting something to stop my thoughts, I joined the local library. I thought reading might help keep them at bay. It was a crime thriller, based on the fact that car satnavs keep a record of the destinations you enter unless you delete them. When Mia told me about Ricky taking Stan and Ollie, the book sprang to mind.

Outside, I race to my car. I can't believe she's agreed so easily. I really thought I was going to have to work on her before she saw the light. I guess telling her about Doctor Saville pushed her over the edge. If I hadn't, she'd have carried on putting up with it until either he convinced her, or killed her.

I doubt he would have walked away. I wouldn't. I think Mia's lovely. When I first got interested in her, I thought she was nothing like me. How wrong I was. We're more alike than either of us could have imagined. In an odd sort of way, I feel an affinity with her, like I did with Camilla. I haven't felt that way with anyone else since.

I always thought she'd be the one who'd have an affair, not Ricky. He always seemed so devoted to her. I guess that's what he wanted people to think. And, boy, was he successful.

Driving out of Knutsford, I stop at some traffic lights. A woman in the car to my left is talking on hands-free. She looks really fired up about something. She catches me watching, glances across and keeps on talking. I wonder what she'd think if she could read my mind. Would she be horrified? Maybe she, too, wants to kill her husband. She's young. Too young to have had her life ripped out and shoved back inside the wrong way round. She doesn't have that haunted look. I could be wrong, of course. Maybe she's miserable but isn't showing it. Maybe she's wrung out, exhausted from burning the candle at both ends trying to be the good wife, the perfect mother. I want to tell her it's not worth it. Women are always trying to please, and in our struggle for approval, we lose part of who we are. The worst part is that we don't even realise we're doing it, until one day something happens and we snap.

Take me, for instance. I'm a prime example. Wife, mother, housekeeper, architect, holiday organiser, party organiser. Christmas, Easter, birthday, any event you can think of, I organised. For years I kept all the plates spinning. Then Frank made them all come crashing down. After that, life was an uphill journey. Getting out of bed was too much effort. Even breathing seemed too hard. You know what they say: forgiveness is the key to moving on. Holding onto hate eats away inside you, they say. Oh, and the one about time being a healer. Well, I'm here to tell you that what they say is a load of bollocks. There is no way forward for people like me. The pain has built up inside me until it's reached breaking point. With or without Mia, there's no turning back.

When I first thought of this plan, I realised it had to be done with someone as desperate as me. I mean, we all think about it sometimes, but actually carrying it out is a whole new ballgame. Mia is going to struggle when it comes to taking the final step, but her problem is much simpler than mine. She only wants to hurt Ricky, whereas I want to lash out at anyone within reach. Why should I be the only person suffering like this? It's unfair.

Suddenly, I can't breathe. I pull in to the side of the road, causing the driver in the car behind me to lean on his horn. I close my eyes and try to calm myself down. *Breathe, breathe*, I tell myself. I lean back against the headrest. This happens out of nowhere, and it's getting worse. It's the thoughts. Every day. From the moment I wake up, I am battling the pictures. The damned pictures. God, I would give anything to stop seeing those damned scenes. That's the problem with thoughts. They're inside your head. Over and over, like some tacky TV re-run, slowly driving me insane. As if knowing it happened isn't hard enough to deal with, I have to keep seeing it too.

I have to speak to them. I have to tell my girls the guilt is too much.

I call Gillian. As always, it goes to voicemail. 'Hello, it's Gillian. Sorry I can't take your call. Leave your name and number and I'll get back to you. If that's you, Mum, I promise I'll call you back as soon as I can.'

'Gillian, I have to speak to you.' My voice cracks. I'm shaking so much I'm in danger of dropping the phone. 'I'm so sorry. I made a mistake. I'm sorry. I wish it was me. I can't stop seeing it. I'm always angry and in so much pain. Oh, God. I'm tired, Gillian. I've exhausted myself trying to keep it together. I need you to understand why I didn't do anything to stop it. I need to know you forgive me. I can't get through to Debra, her phone is dead. I don't know how much longer I can live without seeing you both. Please help me.' Tears pouring down my face, I swallow what seems like a squash ball lodged in my throat. 'I love you both so much.' End call.

* * *

After I've calmed down, I drive off to meet Mia. I will tell her. Not yet, though. But I will when the time is right.

I've no idea if what I'm going to do will make my life any better. Probably not.

It's raining heavily when I pull in to the car park at the gym. I know there's no CCTV here. Mia is already here, waiting for me. She opens her car door, looks around and races towards me. I lean over and open the passenger door. She's wet through after that little stunt. She looks drawn and scared. The glowing look she once had is something from the distant past.

'Have you brought the key?' I ask.

She nods. 'Why do you need it?'

'I'm going to break into his car and get the latest destinations from his satnav.' My chest still hurts and it's hard to breathe normally. She mustn't see how uncomfortable I am. 'His satnav records all the places he's been to. I read it in a novel. You'll have to wait here. You can't risk being seen.'

'He'll go off his head if you damage his car.'

She looks at me. She can tell I've been crying. I look away. 'Well, he won't think it's you, you're supposed to be locked up at home.'

'That's the thing. He'll know by now that I'm not there.'

'That might make him leave early,' I say, 'but he won't go before the awards are announced.'

'Oh God, Lindy, do you really think we'll find Stan and Ollie? What if someone's taken them? You hear stories of pets being stolen and abused.' She covers her face with her hands and cries like a child. 'I couldn't bear it if anything's happened to them.'

I understand how she feels. The cruel bastard. Poor, innocent animals. I put my hand on Mia's. 'We'll find them.' I just hope we can. 'You can't go back home. Did you take the tea towels off the cameras?' She nods. 'Let's hope he thinks there was a blip in the system and stays away tonight. Do you think he will?'

'If he doesn't realise I've gone, he won't come back. He'll probably drink too much at the awards, and he's too mean to get a taxi if he doesn't have to. Plus, he'll want to leave me locked up in my bedroom as long as possible, so I really suffer.'

'OK. Look, I'll go now. We can't lose any more time. Think positive, Mia. Keep in mind what a shit he is and that he's prepared to destroy you to get what he wants.'

She nods, but I can see she's not thinking about anything except Stan and Ollie.

'Call me as soon as you find them, won't you? Please.' She starts to cry again.

'I can't. We need to keep our calls to a minimum. Besides he'll know I've phoned. You haven't brought your phone, have you?' She shakes her head. 'He has your phone linked to his, right?' She nods absently. 'When I find them, where should I take them? To the rescue centre?' I haven't thought this through at all. God, I really need to focus. The wind outside has picked up, and whips up the fallen leaves in a tornado.

'No, they're chipped so they'd call us. Take them to Beth. Here's her address.' She writes it down on a scrap of paper from her handbag. 'Tell her you found them but not what we're planning. Just say . . . Oh, I don't know.'

'I'll tell her it's better not to ask questions,' I say. 'She won't, will she?'

'No, I don't think so. She hates Ricky. She knows what he's done with the dogs. I sort of told her a little about what he's been doing to me, but not much. I haven't mentioned the affair. I kept the really bad stuff to myself. I guess it was a mistake to tell her anything, in view of what we're going to do.'

The weather is getting worse, a storm is gathering. The trees sway back and forth in the wind. I try not to see it as an omen.

'Christ, Mia. She might think you had something to do with it when it all comes out, though it's unlikely. Not if we stick to the plan. We have to stick to the plan at all costs, and you need an alibi. You'll have to use Beth as your alibi. We've already gone off plan. Nobody was supposed to know we are friends. Dammit, she knows I was at the house when you passed out. The good thing is that she's still in the dark about what's really going on with you two.'

'She won't say anything, I'm sure of it.'

'Now, you go to that B&B we spoke about, and keep your head down.'

I don't know how she can be that certain of her sister. I hope she's right. As for me, after two years of being alone in the darkness, I no longer trust anyone.

'How will you get in touch? I don't have my phone.'

'I'll come to you.'

* * *

At nine o'clock I park up outside the venue, outside the range of the security cameras. It's great that it's raining, it means I don't look out of place with my hood up.

I walk through the car park, looking for his car and keeping my eyes peeled for any unexpected security. The car park is full. His car is going to be the last one I come to, just you see, it always is. I keep my head down. Since I'm not going to damage anything they won't bother checking the CCTV. Hopefully, he won't even know I've been in his car. My only worry is that someone might see me getting into it.

The car is in the middle of a row, with a lamp post right in front of it. I pull the key fob from my pocket and press.

There's a click, and the lights flash on and off. I open the door, jump in and put the key in the ignition, turning it once so the engine doesn't start. The navigation system lights up. In the rear-view mirror I see a figure move past, and I swear my heart actually stopped. Once he's gone, I take photos of the destinations, remembering to return the settings to where they were. I turn off the car and slip out, locking it behind me. And notice the wet patch on the seat. Shit. I open up again and wipe it with some tissues from my pocket. Telling myself it's perfectly reasonable to be running in this rain, I race to my car and throw myself in.

I plug the destination into Google Maps on my phone and drive. It's the only place he went that day. I'm taken further away from the main roads, down unsavoury roads with young lads lurking on street corners. Hoods are up. Pedestrians use umbrellas. I mustn't be noticed driving down here. Again, I haven't thought this through. I should have come in daylight.

The rain begins to ease off. Poor Stan and Ollie, they couldn't have waited another day. In the boot I have a large torch I brought from home. A right and then a left leads me to the end of a terraced street. Google maps tells me I'm in Crumpsall, North Manchester. Bastard came a long way to dump the poor things. Doubtless he was hoping that if they did get loose they'd have no chance of finding their way back home.

It's pitch black ahead. The rain has stopped. In the beam from the headlights, I see a patch of waste land and a railway line. Ice cold fingers running down my back, I picture them tied to the tracks.

I stop the car and get out. Take the torch from the boot, switch it on and lock the car. I have some cooked chicken in a bag, a bottle of water in my pocket and a bowl to put it in. My heart in my mouth, I step into the blackness.

I pick my way through heaps of rubbish, tripping on a bicycle wheel and some discarded tin cans. It's a fly tipping zone. I scrabble up the bank towards the railway tracks, shining my torch beam left and right, calling, 'Stan! Ollie!

Stan! Ollie!' My ears strain for the slightest sound, the faintest whimper. What if they're afraid and are skulking somewhere? I might miss them. I hadn't thought of that either.

I come to a partly collapsed fence and graze my ankle climbing over, listening out for oncoming trains.

I stumble over a fallen tree, climb onto it and shine my torch back over the wasteland. Then I hear it. So faint at first I think I've imagined it. Listening hard, I open the bag of cooked chicken in the hopes they'll be able to pick up the scent. They might not be able to come to me but I'm hoping they'll make enough noise for me to know where they are. There it is again. A faint whining in the distance. The memory of another dark night flashes into my mind. I push it away. I hear it again, only this time it's louder and more frantic. Shaking the bag of chicken, I stumble forward, calling out their names. 'Stan! Ollie! Come on, guys, where are you?' I crumple the plastic bag to make some noise, pull out some chicken and wave it around, hoping the wind will carry the scent.

Hearing it again, I set off in the direction I think it's coming from, shining my torch left and right. With no street lights, it's virtually impossible to see anything beyond my torch beam, a couple of feet at most. The light flickers. Oh, no! I realise I've no idea how old the batteries are, and I didn't think to put in new ones. Now I'm in a panic. If I lose the light, I'll be lost too. I pick up my pace, tripping on bricks, cans, and who knows what other detritus. Then I hear a car nearby. I walk faster, my heart pounding in my chest. There's a sound nearby. A rustle. The crunch of footsteps. Someone is walking towards me. I switch off the torch so they don't see me. The footsteps don't seem to be moving towards me. Why? They must be waiting to pounce. I grip the torch tighter. What was I thinking, coming here so unprepared? Now I can't call out to the dogs. I don't want this person getting to them before I do. I press on, trying to move silently.

I should turn back. No. I can't leave the dogs. But I can't lead him to them either. Better go back and come tomorrow in daylight. I stop. He stops. I turn slowly to face the way I came. He moves when I do. Then I hear more movement, slightly further away. There's more than one of them. I'm slightly surprised at how scared I am. I really believed I didn't care what happened to me, and now I find I do. Taking a deep breath, I shine my torch in the direction of the noise. Oh God! It's Stan and Ollie. Their tails wag hesitantly. They don't know me so they're bound to be cautious.

I stumble over to them. Ricky has tied them up with a length of rope. I smother them both with kisses, feed them the chicken. They gobble it up greedily. I put down the bowl and fill it with water. Reassured, they lick me, bump into me, so happy I swear they're smiling.

CHAPTER 18

Mia

Lindy has given me some money to pay for the B&B plus a little extra, so, at 8 a.m., I nip to Boots as soon as it opens. I brought nothing with me when I ran, so there are a few things I need.

I spent the night wondering what Ricky will do when he finds me gone. Maybe this is a mistake and I should go back. He'll definitely tell Sally now. Since we won't be going to the bank, he'll tell her to come home a day early. He'll probably tell my dad to come over at the same time. He and Dr Saville have probably concocted some story about how unhinged I am. She might even have put it in my notes at the surgery.

He's a fool if he thinks he'll get the money that way. But what if I'm deemed incapable of handling my own affairs and he's given power of attorney? That could happen, especially if the good doctor is involved.

I'm surprised how many people come here at this hour. Standing in the queue to pay, I think I recognise the woman in front of me. At the sound of a crying baby, she turns around. With a jolt, I see it's Dr Saville.

Suppose she notices me? She faces forward again. I stand perfectly still, hoping that I'll somehow blend into the background. She's wearing a navy raincoat, double-breasted, with a silk scarf around her neck. She looks elegant, except that her perfume is far too strong.

I wonder how old she is. Is she married? I realise I know nothing about her, and have never been interested, even after I learned of the affair. As a doctor, she's always been professional and considerate. From behind, she looks like she's somewhere in her thirties. Her blonde hair is immaculate, perfectly styled. Does she know what Ricky is doing to me? Probably. She looks the sort. Or does she? Does she look that way to me because I know about the affair?

After she's served, she heads for the door. I drop my items on the nearest shelf and follow her out. What am I doing? Surely I'm not going to confront her? Lindy would. Lindy wouldn't just stand here like a dork and let her get away. I stop her just as she makes her way out. This really isn't a good idea. It will only make Ricky madder, and he'll make me suffer even worse. No he won't. I've left him, haven't I? The thought gives me a burst of energy.

'Oh hello, Dr Saville, I thought it was you.' She stares at me. She obviously doesn't recognise me. I'd forgotten the wig of dark hair Lindy gave me. 'I'm sorry to trouble you . . .' My words trail away. I stand in front of her wondering what to say, while she stares at me blankly. Christ, her skin is quite flawless, she has no wrinkles at all. Funny, I've never really looked at her before. She must be in her very early thirties, if that. She looks toned and athletic. Her full breasts are firm — no sagging there, not like mine.

She smiles politely and waits for me to continue.

'Um, I know I shouldn't approach you like this, away from the surgery, but the sleeping tablets you prescribed for me are too strong. Could you write me a prescription for something else? I can pick them up later.' It's the only thing that comes to mind.

She smiles again. 'I would need to see you at the surgery, Mrs, er . . .'

She's acting as if she doesn't know who I am, but a hard glint in her eyes tells me different. She knows perfectly well that I'm Ricky's wife. 'Mrs Hicks. I think you know my husband, Ricky.' At least she has the grace to blush. 'You could give him the prescription.'

'It's not a problem to change your medication, Mrs Hicks,' she says smoothly, 'but I would need to see you at the surgery. If you can't get an appointment with me, I'm sure one of the other doctors will be able to assist you.'

Crafty. 'Mmm, I suppose, though I'd rather see you, since you're the doctor I usually see.'

She hesitates. 'Well, of course you can, if you're prepared to wait for an appointment, but if you need the pills urgently, you might have to see someone else.'

'Right.' I go to turn around, then stop and face her. 'Since we have a mutual interest in my husband, you might want to fit me in.'

'OK. What exactly are you trying to say, Mrs Hicks?'

'Here? You want us to discuss the matter standing outside Boots?'

'No, of course not. But perhaps you can tell me what you intend doing about this . . . what you think you know.'

'What I think I know? I don't *think* you are fucking my husband, I know you are.'

She sighs. 'All right. Come to the surgery. I'll meet you there in fifteen minutes.'

'No thanks. I don't want to argue with you about it. But know this. I will speak to someone. I'm pretty sure it's against regulations for you to be shagging one of your patients. You know — Hippocratic Oath and all that. You could even lose your licence.' She opens her mouth and closes it again. My insides have turned to water, I need to keep reminding myself that Ricky can't hurt me now.

She turns and clatters away, crashing into another customer who's on their way in. I wonder if she'll ring Ricky straight away, or think it over first. If she's smart, she'll dump him. I doubt the affair's that important to her. I can picture his fury when she does tell him. It makes me smile.

Leaving my shopping where I dumped it, I head for Carphone Warehouse and purchase two pay-as-you-go phones with the cash Lindy gave me. I slipped my own phone into Dr Saville's handbag while I was talking with her. I told Lindy that I hadn't brought it with me. Well, I lied. I'd picked it up at the last minute, thinking I might need it. At least I had switched it off, though I turned it on just before I dropped it into the doctor's handbag.

CHAPTER 19

Lindy

I wake from a nightmare. The house is freezing. I throw on my dressing gown and go downstairs. I can feel it coming on — the darkness. The weight of depression that descends like a black cloud, blocking out everything else. Please, not today. Today, I must be focused.

While I wait for the heating to kick in, I turn on the oven with the door open to warm myself up. I flick on the kettle and drop a teabag into a mug. My grief overwhelms me and I start to cry. The pain will never leave me. The pain is so deep, so agonising I almost howl.

I left the dogs with Beth, giving her the short version of how I'd found them, and that she's not to let Ricky get his hands on them. She wasn't too happy, she was all geared up to go and see him. She only backed down when I told her about Mia. Then, of course, Beth wanted to know where she was. 'For obvious reasons,' I say, 'I can't tell you right now. You'll just have to be patient.' I hadn't wanted anyone to know I was this friendly with Mia, but we don't have a choice. We need Beth right now. I only hope she can keep her mouth shut.

'In hiding?' she says. 'That doesn't sound right. What are you keeping from me?'

I'm sorry I can't tell her, because she cares about her sister. But Mia doesn't want anyone knowing about Sally and her uncle. It's up to her to tell her sister if she wants her to know.

I make tea. The kitchen is starting to warm up but I leave the oven on to speed things on.

I'm calling in sick today. I want the time to myself in order to think things through. I promise Mia I'll get in touch with her this morning. She's been at a B&B overnight, and I've booked her into a hotel some distance away. If anyone asks, she can say she's treating herself to some rest and relaxation — the hotel has a spa.

Two framed photos of Gillian and Debra sit on the windowsill. I run my finger over their faces, wishing they were here so I could explain why I have to do what I'm about to do. 'I know you won't understand, so maybe it's best I don't tell you,' I say to them. They love their father, but he's caused me too much pain. I can't stand the pitying look in his eyes, the way he rests his large hand on my shoulder for a moment as I pass him by. I don't want his pity. He has no idea what I am going through. How could he?

I look at the clock. Gillian will be up by now, so I call her, leaving a message on her voicemail. 'Hi, it's me, Mom. I'm sorry, I know you're always in a rush in the morning. I just need to talk to you and I know you can't come over. Just a quick word, honey. I want to ask you to forgive me for what I'm about to do. I know you love your father, but he did something terrible, and he made me do something terrible too, and I can't forgive him for that. And I can't forgive myself for letting him push me into saying the words that made it all happen.'

I lean my forehead against the windowpane. I've been in such agony for so long I've forgotten what life was like without it. 'I just need to hear your voice, for you to say it's all right, that you understand me and why I have to do this. No, don't try and change my mind. It's all made up.'

It's a relief to tell Gillian how I feel. I wipe my eyes and sit down, staring out of the window into the dark. It's very early, the sun not yet risen, but I can see lights going on in the houses around us as people get ready for work.

I finish my tea and tiptoe upstairs, so as not to wake Frank. I get dressed and put my boots on in the kitchen. I remember to turn off the oven before I go out, closing the front door behind me with a quiet click. I pull my hood up and walk to the bus stop. Two men with shaven heads are waiting for the bus. I keep my head down.

I hadn't reckoned on all the traffic. The cars drive through the puddles, I'm sure they're splashing us on purpose. I take a step back.

The number thirty bus finally arrives. I keep my head down while I buy my ticket, and sit at the back with my hood still up, looking down at my phone. The bus bumps along, lurching over potholes, pulling up to the stops with a gasp.

After what seems an age, I arrive at the stop nearest the B&B. I jump out and walk along St Stephen's Road to the roundabout opposite. This roundabout is a nightmare to cross in the rush hour. There's nobody at the desk at the B&B, so I make my way straight upstairs to her room.

What you plan in your head never turns out like you wanted. The plan in your head never goes wrong. I have brought a bag of food for her, which I set down on the floor. 'Here. Some juice and croissants. I thought you probably hadn't been out and got anything in case you were seen.'

She looks down. 'I, er, did go out, earlier this morning.'

'But I told you not to!'

'Well, I had to get some things from Boots. Then I had to get the phones like you asked. Don't look at me like that — I didn't have a thing. No toothpaste, no deodorant—'

I hold my hand up. 'OK, OK. I hope at least you remembered to wear the wig.'

'I did wear the wig, but I, er, still haven't got the things.'

'How come?' I say.

'I came across Dr Saville in Boots, and I confronted her. I couldn't help myself. Look, I know it was a stupid thing to do—'

'So why did you do it? Are you out of your fucking mind? Now she'll know you have a motive.'

'Stop yelling at me. I didn't plan to tell her. It was just seeing her there. It took me by surprise.'

'And did I hear you say you were wearing the wig? I got that wrong, didn't I? Please tell me I did.'

'No, you heard right. I was wearing it.'

I fling the bag containing her breakfast across the room. 'Fuck! You couldn't have done more damage if you'd tried! Shit!' I get up and stride over to the window. I need to think. 'Right. Listen. This is what we'll do. When the police speak to you — which they will — you'll have to deny having spoken to her. Do you hear me? The police are bound to learn about the affair and, hopefully, they'll think she's lying about it. You will have to insist that you didn't know. Do you hear me, Mia? Don't fuck this up. And you were at the house all night, you only left today to go to the spa hotel.'

Picking the bag up, I hand it over to her with a glass from the bedside table for the juice. Back at the window, I stand and look out. It's happening. It's going to work. I watch people going about their business and wonder if the world will look any different once we've done it.

I remember my promise to tell Mia my story. The thought makes my throat constrict. I'm not doing it here, in this non-descript little room.

I tell Mia to eat her breakfast and get dressed. We're going out.

'To the hotel? Isn't it a bit early?'

'No, not the hotel. I said I was going to tell you what made me want to . . . well, do what we're doing, but I need to take you somewhere first.'

'OK. So where are we going?'

'We have to catch a bus. I didn't bring my car, there's too many CCTV cameras around. Keep your hood up. You paid cash for the room on arrival, didn't you? And told them you were leaving early because you had a plane to catch?'

She nods. 'I look so different in this black wig.'

It doesn't suit her at all. 'That's the idea. I can't imagine what that Saville woman thought when she saw you wearing that thing. When you get to the hotel, check in looking like you normally do. Lose the wig. Dump it before you arrive.'

'Are you sure Ricky won't find me there?'

'I don't think he'll start ringing the hotels, there's too many of them. No, he'll start with your friends. He'll most likely go to Beth's first. I have a feeling he'll want to tell her about Sally, so I need to get back to your house and stop him leaving. Ring the hotel where he's staying. Tell them you're his wife and ask if he's still there.'

Mia looks scared. 'Do I have to?'

'Yes. We need to know how much time we have.'

'How will you do it?' she says anxiously. 'What if he went back there last night?'

'The last thing he'd have expected was for you to escape. And it's best you don't know anything about it, then you can't give anything away when the police question you. Remember what I said. You are going to the spa to chill out, because you're run down. Everyone says how thin and tired you look, so we'll play on that. Ricky stayed at the hotel last night, and he said he'd be home today. That's all you need to know.'

'Lindy, I . . . I'm not sure that this is the right thing to do. I mean suppose we get caught. I—'

I round on her. 'Shut up, Mia. It's too late to back out now. Anyway, where could you go? Have you forgotten how he's been treating you? What he's going to do to your family? Have you? You think he should get away with that?' She shakes her head. 'I thought not. So trust me. There's nothing to connect us with what's going to happen.'

'I don't think I can hurt anyone. When the moment arrives, I won't be able to go through with it.'

'Yes, you will. Now shut up and let's go.'

CHAPTER 20

Mia

I hurt my hand trying to get it under the door.

It's nothing compared to the dread in the pit of my stomach. That's agonising. The whole thing is madness. Now that I'm away from Ricky and no longer living in fear of his violence, it all seems absurd. Why did I agree to her plan? What was I thinking?

She looks drawn and weary, her skin has an unhealthy pallor. According to her, I'm supposed to book myself into this hotel and make use of the spa while she goes back to my house to murder my husband. It's insane. She's insane.

She won't even tell me when or how she's going to do it, in case I trip up when the police question me. The police! They'll know I'm lying. They're not stupid.

I feel sick. The croissant sits in its brown paper bag, uneaten. I can't face it.

I keep telling her I can't go through with it but she's not listening. It's as if she's in a different world. I can't seem to reach her.

Getting rid of Ricky had seemed like the solution to all my problems. Simple, right? But murder? There has to be another way. Nothing is worth murdering someone for, even hurting my family. Christ. The ramifications will be far worse than what he's going to do to them. I could go to prison.

'Look, Mia, you were in despair yesterday. Have you forgotten that? Have you forgotten what he's done to you? Look what he did to your dogs. He'll have caused you a great deal more pain than that by the time he's finished with you. And I mean finished. You told me he's alluded to it. He's obsessed with getting your money. Even if you give it to him, he's going to tell Sally anyway. He's said so. He's put it all in motion, for fuck's sake. What do you need to happen before you see that the bastard is going to stop at nothing to destroy you, including killing you if you get in his way? So, unless you're prepared to allow him to destroy Sally's life, along with your entire family, I don't see what choice you have.'

'There's always a choice,' I yell back at her.

'No, there isn't, and besides, you promised me you would go through with it. You can't back out now.'

'Look.' Now I'm clutching at straws. 'Maybe if we sit down with Ricky and tell him he can have the money, but he has to sign some sort of legally binding agreement not to speak out. He might agree.'

'I thought you were smarter than that, Mia. Clearly, I was wrong.' She turns and stands facing me. 'So. Tell me how that's going to pan out. He gets the money which your grandparents left for the girls and buggers off into the sunset with his doctor shag. Then he decides to rip your life apart anyway and tells Sally and your dad. The damage is done! Agreement or no agreement, he'll tie you up in court for ages, and in the meantime your family is in tatters. And so are you.'

She is set on going through with this. Nothing I say will change her mind.

'Neither of us can incriminate the other,' she continues. 'We cannot be seen together after today. That is why you have to go to the hotel.'

'Why me? Why me, Lindy? Do I look like the type of woman who'd commit murder?'

She smiles and sits down on the end of the bed. 'I wasn't thinking of that in the beginning. When I first saw you, you looked happy, free spirited, and, supposedly, so very in love with your husband. I was fascinated by you. I followed you everywhere until I knew as much about you as any person outside of your family could know.' She shrugs. 'I guess I was stalking you, but in a good way.' Lindy peels a layer of pastry off the croissant and eats it. She hasn't answered my question. 'If you mess up, we both go down together. You know that, right?'

She won't accept the fact that I'm not going through with it. That I can't. Murder? That's what gangsters do. Bad people. Not me. I'm a housewife. A mother. A gym teacher, for goodness sake.

'As I was saying, in the beginning I wasn't thinking of anything definite. It was a sort of fantasy. I knew I wanted to get rid of Frank, but I hadn't worked out how. I guess the plan had been germinating in my subconscious and you just happened to bring it to life.'

I had looked on Lindy as my saviour. Now she looked more like my tormentor.

'Why do you want to kill Frank? You still haven't told me,' I say.

She clenches her fists. 'Like I said, I can't do it here. If you want to know why, then we have to leave now. Come on.'

She grabs my arm. I draw back. 'Lindy, I'm not going through with this. I won't go to jail, not for you or anyone else.'

'Yes, you will, because when I kill Ricky, I will make sure to obtain evidence that points the finger at you. And if you refuse to carry out your part, I will release it to the police. Did you really think I wouldn't have taken that into account?'

CHAPTER 21

Lindy

Thankfully, Mia is silent during the bus ride. I keep looking at my watch. It's still early, and I'm counting on Ricky being hungover and too shagged out to go home in a hurry. Supposedly locked up in the house, Mia will be the last thing on his mind. I heard on the radio that he won an award. He'll have celebrated hard last night.

The closer we get to our destination, the more anxious I feel. As the memories rise to the surface and the images grow clearer, my chest starts to ache. Tears run down my cheeks. I can't stop them. I turn to face the window. Mia puts her hand on my back, but I shrug it off. I don't want her sympathy.

'Lindy, are you all right? Can I help?' No, she can't. No one can help me. No one.

Abruptly, I jump up and make for the door and press the bell. The bus lurches to a stop and I jump out, Mia following. I stride off, with her trailing after me, her words of comfort and reassurance blowing away in the freshening breeze. Useless words. She should see what I see.

We're getting closer now. Crossing the road, we pass a man walking his two dogs; one has a stick in its mouth.

He glances at the two of us — we must look a bit odd, me marching towards the cemetery with Mia in my wake. Inside, beneath a canopy of trees swaying in the wind, the path threads between the graves.

Mia slows her pace, increasing the distance between us. 'What are we doing here, Lindy?'

I can't speak. I grab her hand and pull her along the familiar path. A left, then a right, and then I come to a halt. Both of us are panting from the exertion.

We stand in a carpet of leaves. The faint smell of a coal fire drifts through the trees. I bend down and sweep fallen leaves from the headstones. The flowers in the two brass vases are dead. They don't last long this time of year. With a finger I trace the letters on the headstones. I speak to them, telling them I'm here, watching over them. I tell them I'll never forget.

Gillian Annie Villas and Debra Victoria Villas.

I bow my head and ask them for forgiveness. Tell them how sorry I am for not watching out for them. I fall silent. The breeze has ceased to blow and in the stillness I can hear the faint scratch of a beetle trundling across one of the stones.

I sense Mia crouching at my back. She places a hand on my shoulder. Her touch causes the tears to flow.

'I don't know what to say to you, Lindy. You . . . you always made out they were alive and just living away. I'm so sorry.' Her voice is gentle, full of compassion. She reaches out for my hand and takes it in hers. 'I can't begin to understand how you must feel, I'm just so, so sorry.'

I've never been able to stand people's sympathy. Suddenly angry, I scramble to my feet. I yell at her, 'No, you can't understand. No one can!' No one understands about the pain. The pain, like an evil monster at my back that never leaves me, that never allows me to escape.

'They — my girls — they didn't just die. They didn't get an infection, they didn't drown, or fall off a cliff. They died in a horrific road accident that *I* could have prevented. Me, their mother! I failed them. I knew Frank shouldn't have been driving when he'd had so much to drink.

'Instead of stopping him, I waved them off. Know where to? To the fucking services to buy me a bottle of wine! You're asking why. Well, they thought it would help me because I'd just had my precious little dog put down. She had cancer. I went to get the one bottle we had in the house and found that Frank had drunk it. When she saw how low and pissed off I was, Gillian suggested going for another bottle. Sweet Gillian. She offered to get me some chocolate while they were there.

'Fucking Frank was so keen to show off the new swanky car he'd picked up the day before, he said he'd drive them, despite my protests. I knew they'd have to go via the motorway to get there, and I wasn't happy about it. He'd just finished a whole bottle of wine and was way over the limit. The girls told me I was too prissy about drinking and driving. They said Dad had just eaten a big dinner and was fine.

'So I let them go. I fucking waved.

'Frank pulled onto the motorway from the slip road in front of an articulated lorry. It smashed into them, pushing the car into another lorry just ahead. Debra was thrown forward from the back seat, and Gillian—'

'What, Lindy? What about Gillian?' Mia breathes.

'Gillian wasn't wearing her seat belt.' I groan. 'She was decapitated. The police said the seatbelt wouldn't have helped her anyway. But I . . . I keep seeing her without her head.'

'But Frank survived? How?' Mia says.

'God knows. Maybe God thought it was a huge joke, letting him live. Believe in God, Mia, do you? I don't. They call God the merciful, don't they, so how could he have allowed this to happen? Frank was thrown from the car. He broke both legs, his collarbone and his hip. But he lived. I hate him for that. I hate him for being alive. I hate myself, too. I knew he shouldn't have got in that car. I should have stopped him, but I didn't. So it's my fault they died.' I am on my knees now, weeping uncontrollably, while Mia holds me in her arms.

'It was months before I could even speak. I was in a mental hospital for a long time. They gave me drugs to help me sleep and drugs to get me through the day. But no drugs could stop me seeing their mangled bodies. Seeing my beautiful daughter without her head.'

Mia is crying too now. 'I went to the crash site. The car was so compressed it looked like a giant had picked it up and squashed it like an empty tin can. They'd got them out by then. It took them hours, apparently. They had to carry me away. At the funeral they had to have closed coffins. People were whispering about Gillian and her head.'

Exhausted, I slump against Mia and let her rock me.

She is the first person I've told, and I feel a bit bad about laying it on her. 'Sorry,' I say. 'I needn't have given you all the details.'

'It's all right, Lindy,' she says softly. 'I hope telling someone about it has helped, a little at least.'

We sit in silence for a while until I pull myself together. 'We have to go, we've spent far too much time here.'

I see her hesitate. Surely she's not going to back down now? Not after what I've told her. 'Mia,' I say, 'you have a daughter too. Even if I didn't stop my girls being . . . hurt, you can keep her from being harmed.' Finally, it dawns on me that Mia is nothing like me. I thought hearing my story would change her mind. It hasn't. She's not going to go through with it. She's going to try and stop me.

CHAPTER 22

Mia

I keep thinking of how I can put a stop to this. I now understand why Lindy is the way she is, but it doesn't make it any better. It is madness to even think of murdering Ricky and Frank. I can't do it. I was a fool to go along with it in the first place.

I've agreed to go to the spa hotel simply because I can't think of anywhere else to go. I'm afraid to face Ricky but I know I will have to in the end. There is no other way.

After the first treatment, I check myself out. I cannot believe he will hurt his daughter. He's been a good parent and Sally adores him. This is so fucked up. I've fucked up. I've put money before the girls.

I told Lindy I won't go through with her plan, and that if she does what she threatens, I will go to the police. We argued all the way to the hotel, where she left me at the door and stormed off. I just hope she's realised what a stupid plan it was, and how out of control she has become. I want to help her, but not this way.

I can't believe I ever agreed to it in the first place. Ricky has done terrible things to me, but I have to think of Sally. I can take anything he throws at me, but I can't take her pain. The fear of her getting hurt because I tried to hold onto the money is almost too much to bear. My stubbornness has got me into hot water before. If I'd just agreed in the first place, like a regular person with a brain, Ricky wouldn't have gone to such extremes. I want him out of my life, but not dead. I have to believe he won't hurt her. I know he loves her, and I'm convinced he still thinks of her as his daughter. And if in the end he does tell her, I will just have to face the consequences.

So now I'm waiting at reception for a taxi to take me home.

CHAPTER 23

Lindy

When I arrive at Mia's house, Ricky's not yet back. I park on a street a good distance away and walk to their house with my coat buttoned up and my hood pulled over my face. The fur collar helps.

It's a miserable day. The sky is full of heavy dark clouds. The wind picks up rubbish; a plastic bottle is rolling down the street. It's bin day. The bin men have been round, and the empty ones shunt around the pavement, or lean together like drunken robots. I hold my hood tight at the neck to stop it blowing off and turn into Mia's drive.

I walk in through the garage, the way Mia escaped, slipping into her house through the integrated kitchen door. Inside, I pull off my boots and coat, shoving them into the cupboard under the stairs. I check the floor for footprints.

I know just what I'm going to do to him. I've thought it all out, long and hard. It's a little crazy — no, it's a lot crazy. I'm going to have to be really fast to succeed.

Ricky deserves it. He's an arrogant son of a bitch. He too thinks drink driving a short distance is safe. He's lucky he hasn't hit anyone. Yet. The thought makes me angry, my rage takes shape. A poisoned arrow, aimed straight at him.

Of course, it's Frank I really want to kill, not this comparative stranger. Trouble is, the finger would immediately be pointed at me. Everyone knows our story, and my subsequent mental breakdown. We had it all, Frank and me. But he left me with nothing. I want satisfaction. An eye for an eye. Will I feel better when he's dead? Maybe not. Probably not. Nothing will bring back my girls. But I can't stand the fact that he's alive and they're not.

We were a close family. Even after they left home, I called them every day. Now all I have is their voicemail. I still pay for their mobile contracts, I can't bear to cancel them. You probably think that's sick, but it means I can still hear their voices. I can even hear them breathing.

Frank and I were a good-looking couple and our daughters took after us. People used to stare at us enviously when we all went out, and the girls always had admirers. I was so proud of them.

Frank attracted me with his looks and his confidence. He made me feel safe, protected. Little did I know. I'll certainly never trust anyone again. I push the thoughts from my head. I have a job to do.

I know I'm taking a risk. Mia says she's not going through with it. She will. Once Ricky is dead. I have her recorded on my phone, agreeing to it, saying she wants him dead. If I have to, I will use it to blackmail her.

It's all happening too quickly for Mia. As for me, it feels like I've been playing with the idea for an eternity. I know it's crazy. In my heart of hearts I know it will solve nothing. I just have to do it. I can't not do it.

How cold I've become. I feel no remorse about what I'm about to do.

I check I have everything I need. According to Mia, he'll come straight upstairs to look for her. He'll rush upstairs, open the bedroom door and see that she's not there. He'll never figure out how she escaped. I must say I was impressed with her resourcefulness.

Ricky isn't the type to panic. He'll assume she's gone to Beth's. He'll phone her with some story, not wanting to arouse her suspicions. When he's established she's not there, he will try her friends. When he finds she's not with any of them, he will think of me.

With no idea where I live, I'm guessing he'll google me, or look me up on the open register. We're not on it. I took us off when it all happened. There were too many creeps looking to seek us out so they could hear all the gory details. Sick bastards . . .

The key turns in the front door lock.

CHAPTER 24

Mia

I arrive at my house to find the front door wide open. Ricky's car is in the drive. The house is silent. At 5.30 p.m. it's already dark. The taxi has gone, its headlights disappearing down the street, and I am alone in the pitch black night.

The porch light is the only light on in the house. It casts a shadow over the entrance like a gaping mouth waiting to swallow me up.

Slowly, I approach the open door. Why has Ricky left it open like this? He never leaves it open. My pulse races. He knows I've escaped. He'll be waiting for me inside the door. What will he do to me?

Taking a deep breath, I walk in anyway. No one there. All my earlier bravado is fast evaporating, leaving me doubting the wisdom of ever coming back.

Hesitantly, I call out. 'Ricky? Ricky, are you there?' My heart in my mouth, I walk through the house, turning the lights on as I go. He will be beside himself with rage that I dared leave the house. I need to tell him what I've decided so we can move on.

'Look, why don't you come out. I want to talk to you.'

Silence.

'Ricky, please, just let me explain. I've decided to let you have the money, all of it. We can go to the bank tomorrow like you said, and put your name on the account.'

There is no answer.

Drawn to the pantry, I open the door. It's empty. A long-handled broom topples against me. I squeal and jump backwards, catching my hip on the edge of the granite worktop.

Rubbing my hip, I pad out of the kitchen towards the stairs, stopping at the cloakroom.

The door is ajar.

Any second now he's going to come running towards me, his face contorted with anger, murder on his mind. I have to speak to him.

'Ricky, are you in there? Look, stop playing games. I've said I'll let you have the money. Take it. I don't want it. I'm sorry if I've been difficult about it. I know I've behaved stupidly. Why don't we put all this behind us? I won't tell anyone about what you . . . about what's been going on. I just want you to promise not to say anything to Sally or Dad. Then all this madness can stop.'

I take another step towards the cloakroom. I open my mouth to speak, and then I see it.

The coat. Lying on the floor. She's left it there for me to find. On top of it is my phone, with a note attached: *Check your voicemail.*

Gingerly, I pick up the pay-as-you-go phone as if it's a ticking bomb. I navigate to voicemail and listen.

I listen to myself telling Lindy I want to kill Ricky. It's all there, my voice, loud and clear and damning. I'm admitting my intent to murder.

How did we get to this point, me and Lindy?

I thought I had put a stop to this crazy scheme of hers. I thought she'd seen sense.

The phone in my pocket is vibrating. I pull it out slowly. A new message. I don't want to see it.

I could go to prison. If I don't carry out my side of the bargain, she will make it look as if it was me who killed my husband. I can't think straight. My girls! They'll think their mother is a murderess. And what if Dr Saville comes forward and testifies? She'll tell them about how I threatened her outside the shop, with that crazy wig on my head.

I was delusional in even considering this idea. Now I realise I was even more delusional in thinking I could walk away.

I pocket the phone and, legs shaking, I hang onto the banister and start to mount the stairs. Each step increases my dread. The phone vibrates again, and again. I can't look at it now. My whole being is focused on getting up these stairs. I have to know.

As if I don't already. Ricky wouldn't keep me waiting like this if something wasn't wrong with him. I know him. He wouldn't be capable of holding back this long.

The phone keeps vibrating.

As I near the top of the stairs, I see the heavy brass lamp-stand lying on its side on the landing.

Only four more steps to go. I hear my daughter's voice, accusing me of murder. In trying to protect her, I have made her situation a thousand times worse. This thought's enough to make me stop. I take the phone out of my pocket and open the messages — five of them:

Nothing is worth more than your daughters.

Play along or pay the ultimate price.

Your future has been changed. You cannot go back.

A promise is a binding oath.

Mia! I'm sorry. I'm sorry. Please forgive me. I'm sorry.

I stare at the phone. She's done it, and now I have to keep my part of the bargain. *Please God, let me be mistaken! I never meant this to happen, I wasn't thinking when I agreed. I never wanted to kill him, I only wanted him out of my life.*

I sit on the stairs, read the last message again and look up at the fallen lampstand.

CHAPTER 25

Lindy

From the kitchen window, I watch Mia enter her house. Concealed behind the open door of the pantry, I listen to her slow progress through the ground floor rooms and up the stairs, to where Ricky is lying. Her shock when she finds him will work to my advantage — the police will be more likely to believe her.

I want to tell her it was a mistake, that somehow it all got out of hand. Too late for that now. I wonder how she reacted to the text messages I sent her. I wish I could take them back. Poor Mia, she didn't deserve any of this. I hope to God she's strong enough to go through with it.

Once she's gone up the stairs, I go back and collect my coat. Pity I can't stay and watch her reaction. Reluctantly, I go out through the back door and slip away into the night.

He was stronger than I'd expected but I had the advantage of surprise. That, and the fact that I didn't give a stuff about what might happen to me.

He whined like a dog. Appropriate, really, considering what he'd done to Stan and Ollie.

I taunted him. I wanted him trembling and weak with fear. He laughed when he first saw me; he's always considered me more than a little loopy. He called me a mad cow. Then he saw the knife.

'Never heard the saying, "beware of the lunatics"?' I say, waving the knife in front of his face. I was in a sort of miasma at that point and even I knew I wasn't making any sense.

Ricky watched me, eyes narrowed and glittering, calculating his next move. He still thought he could overpower me. Big mistake, that.

What Ricky didn't know was that guilt had made me reckless. My courage had failed me once — on that fatal night when I let Frank drive away with my lovely daughters. It wasn't going to fail me now.

I take a step forward. Ricky backs away. Isolated memories of that night flit through my mind like scraps from a torn-up picture. The knock on the front door, and my shock at finding two police officers there. 'Mrs Villas, I'm afraid there has been an accident. Perhaps you should sit down.' The male officer brings me a glass of water.

I hear myself screaming. I see myself running to the front door, saying I have to get to them. I feel them take hold of me, feel myself struggle to break free. I gave them the slip, though. I scratched and bit. I remember snatching up my car keys and driving to the motorway. Leaving the engine running, I jumped out of the car and raced towards the flashing lights of the emergency vehicles. I managed to slip through the crowd surrounding the wrecked vehicles until an officer stopped me. When I told them who I was, he pulled me back, saying, 'You shouldn't be here.' As I was dragged away, I caught a glimpse of Frank, lying on the ground.

I saw him move.

He was the only survivor.

Sitting in the back of an ambulance, a foil blanket draped over my shoulders, I heard them talking amongst themselves. Shaking his head, one of them said the word, 'Decapitated.'

After that, everything went black. I came to in a psychiatric ward. For a long time I didn't speak. I refused to eat. They fed me like a child. Heavily sedated, I wandered the corridors. I remained in that place for a year.

Now I'm back in the world I'm surprised I've managed to hold down a job and be half courteous to people. Every day, I live with the flashbacks, the burning acrid smell from the smashed-up vehicles. The images never fade.

It should be Frank here now, not greedy Dicky Ricky. Maybe I'm being cowardly in taking my revenge this way. As I grapple with the ghosts from my past, I hear him speaking. He sounds cocky. He sneers.

'And just what do you think you're going to do with that?' He jerks his head toward the knife.

'I'm going to kill you.'

He laughs.

It's enough to focus my mind. The plan, I think. Intruder enters house, disturbs owner and kills him. Simple.

I can't concentrate. What am I doing here? This is all wrong. Killing this man isn't going to make anything better. After all, I was just as responsible as Frank. I knew he was over the limit, yet I let him drive. I should never have let him push me around. And who am I to think I have a monopoly on pain and sorrow? Other people have suffered losses too.

It isn't Frank's fault that he survived. Sure, he prepared the bomb, laid the fuse, but I lit the match. I was the one who let him get in that car and drive away.

I stand, poised between two alternatives. Kill him — or, what? I have gone over this in my head a thousand times. I see Frank's face superimposed on Ricky's. Why did he survive?

The knife trembles slightly in my hand. I'm beginning to sweat.

This is wrong.

Ricky is a shit for treating Mia the way he has, but it is not for me to decide who lives and who dies.

I don't have that power.

I am wrong to think I can kill someone just because they caused an accident.

Then Ricky makes a move. He steps forward.

Everything's happening too fast.

I'm not ready.

'My daughters are dead,' I say. It's the first time I have ever said it aloud. The words seem to echo around this featureless room. Maybe it's my girls, telling me not to do this.

'Well,' he says, 'I've met a ton of crazy people in my business but you're off the scale.'

His eyes travel from my face to the knife. I grip it tighter. I've lost my nerve. My throat closes up.

'Do you really think you're going to stab me with that knife? You really are dumb, aren't you?'

Yes, I'm dumb. And this is a dumb idea.

He sneers. 'Just like those dogs. They were so willing to go with me. Stupid animals. I was going to break their back legs just for the hell of it. It would really kill Mia to see them that way. I don't know why I didn't. I think I'll go back there after I've finished with you, and film myself doing it. Pay Mia back for sending you to kill me for her.'

He really shouldn't have said that.

I pull back my arm and bring it forward. The knife blade goes straight through him. After a slight resistance as it presses on the skin, it travels in smoothly. I am surprised to see how much of the knife has disappeared inside him.

Dazed, I stand there while Ricky gradually slumps forward against me. Disgusted, I push him off. He stumbles against the banister rail at the top of the stairs. He's in danger of falling.

He's blocking my way. I can't get past him.

Then he makes a lurch for me. I jump clear and race down the stairs. Wait. He's not dead. He was supposed to die. I rush back up.

He can't live. He'll talk. He'll tell the police it was me.

Oh shit.

How come he's not dead? I fucking stabbed him, for God's sake. Now I see. I stabbed him in the side. It's just a flesh wound. I'll be arrested. He'll get away with everything. The dogs are worrying me a lot. He'll take them from Beth's. I can't let him break their legs.

I have to finish this.

My breath is coming in short, sharp gasps.

He's got to his feet. I edge round him, my back against the wall.

My clothes are sticking to my back. Sweat trickles between my breasts. I can't let him get away.

He pulls the knife out of his side and cries out in pain. Blood pours from the wound. A lot of it. He really shouldn't have done that.

The knife in his hand, he takes a step towards me. He's going to kill me.

I find I don't want to die after all. He'll destroy both of us, Mia and I. I don't have a choice. I step back, knocking against a lampstand. A big heavy lamp, with a solid brass base. A weapon.

He looks into my eyes. He's losing a lot of blood. Growing weaker by the second. He's going to die but he can still hurt me first. He has the knife. He has me pinned to the wall.

My hand closes around the lamp.

'You missed your chance,' he says, his breath coming in shallow gasps. His face is white. Where he gets the strength from I don't know, but he lunges forward, catching me off guard.

He crashes against me, landing on top of me. I feel around for the lamp, which is just out of reach. I hear the knife land on the floor as his hands go around my throat. His grip tightens. 'Arsehole,' I gasp. 'I know what you did to her. She told me what you threatened to do to your daughter.'

'You don't know what you're talking about,' he whispers hoarsely. 'Well, I'll tell you how this is going to go. Lunatic intruder tries to kill house owner who defends himself after near fatal stabbing. Naturally, they'll believe me. Your doctor told me all about your time in the nuthouse.'

He's squeezing harder. I'm beginning to choke. My fingers strain to reach the lamp. Just another inch. Then what? It's too heavy to pick up with my fingers. He relaxes his hold slightly. I gasp for breath. 'Now. Tell me where she is.'

I need to get my whole hand round it. 'She's with Beth. The dogs are too, we found them. Beth knows everything. You can't hide. Beth will tell the world what you've done to her sister.' His grip tightens again. I turn my head from left to right. 'She loved you. Then you had to go and spoil it with that tramp of a doctor.' I can't breathe. I'm blacking out, lights dance in front of my eyes. I don't want to die.

'She should have given me the money. I would have walked away then. Beth won't tell.' He laughs. 'She won't want to hurt her family. They're very close, you know.'

I gag. 'You're willing to destroy your daughter for money.'

His grip loosens imperceptibly. 'The point is, she should have told me in the beginning. She lied. Our whole marriage was a lie.'

'She loved you. Your daughters still love you. You raised them, they're yours.'

The effort of speaking has taken all my strength.

The faces of my two beautiful girls rise up in front of my eyes. They're urging me to fight. At last, I pull my hand from beneath him. I scratch at his face. Claw at his eyes. He turns his head away, and in doing so his grip on my throat loosens enough for me to take in a gulp of air.

I stick my fingers in his eyes and press. He yells, releasing his hold from around my throat to grab at my hand. Now I can reach the lamp. He staggers back, hands over his eyes.

I grab hold of the lamp and lift it up, slamming the base into his head with all my strength. Ricky rolls over once and lies still.

I step over both lamp and Ricky, trying not to look at him. Blood flows from his head in a slowly expanding pool.

As I get to my feet something latches onto my ankle. I scream. It's his hand.

I kick him, hard, with my other foot. So hard my toes hurt. He groans, and the hand falls away.

Free, I spin around. I am just about to go down the stairs when, to my horror, I see him getting to his feet. The knife is back in his hand. Blood pours from the wound on his head. How can he possibly be alive?

Frozen, terrified, I watch Ricky, his face the colour of parchment, pick up the lamp and charge towards me. He's like the bloody Terminator. I throw myself to the side just as he brings the lamp down, striking the wall where I was standing. It hits the wall then bounces on the floor.

Galvanised by my lucky escape, I charge at him, head forward, like a bull in the ring. I ram my head into his chest. He staggers and falls, his head catching the edge of the lamp base.

His eyes stare up at me. He's on his back, unmoving.

This time he's not getting up.

Moving past him, I inch my painful way downstairs. When I reach the kitchen, I pull out my phone and call Mia. Her phone's switched off.

I send her a text: *Mia! I'm sorry. I'm sorry. Forgive me. I'm so sorry.*

CHAPTER 26

Mia

I put my hand to my mouth. The landing carpet is soaked with blood. A large kitchen knife lies next to Ricky who's lying on his back, staring up. One leg is bent beneath him. There's blood on the walls. She'd said it wouldn't be messy. Said she had a plan and it would all be straightforward.

It doesn't look straightforward to me.

I need to call the police. First, I call Lindy.

'This wasn't supposed to happen. I told you no. Why didn't you listen? You went ahead anyway, and now it's all a mess!'

Gently, calmly, Lindy reassures me that all will be well. I have an alibi. I'm safe. They can't blame me, nobody knows he was abusing me. Only Beth, and Lindy is certain she can persuade her to keep quiet.

She sounds so confident. Already, I can hear police sirens in the distance. She tells me to get rid of the pay-as-you-go phone and hangs up.

* * *

Police line the street. Reporters block the pavements and the entrance to the estate. Sally and Annie, followed by my parents, fight their way through the crowd. It's a big news story — popular TV presenter murdered by an intruder.

Microphones are shoved in front of the girls' faces. 'How do you feel about your father being killed, Miss?' 'Will you ever feel safe in your parents' house again?' 'Do you think they were looking for anything in particular?' I watch from the small window in the utility room. I've been holed up in here since the police arrived and the CSI took some DNA samples from me.

It's bin day again. They're all out except ours. Someone has knocked over the neighbour's. Their rubbish is scattered all over the lawn.

They're all out, the neighbours, agog to hear the details.

My mobile phone rings. One of the television companies wants my exclusive. They're offering a ton of money. I end the call and put my phone on silent.

My father finds me first. He puts his arms around me. He says how sorry they all are and what a loss this is. He says they're there for me. When I hug him back there is the familiar smell of the cigars he likes so much. He rubs my back while I weep into his neck, as if I'm a little girl once again and Daddy is consoling me following a fall. I think of his brother and the lie I've kept from him all these years. I want to tell him that, frankly, Ricky deserved it. He had it coming, but it wasn't me who killed him.

I don't say much. I'm terrified to even open my mouth in case I say something to drop us in it. The police put it down to shock.

'When I came home I thought it was odd that Ricky was back early and had left the front door open. I called out but he didn't answer. The house was too quiet. I had a feeling something was wrong.'

At first, I say, I thought he must be in the shower and couldn't hear me. 'But something felt off, and I became uneasy.' *Dammit, why did I say that?*

The police sergeant picks up on it immediately. 'Was there anything specific that made you feel uneasy? Did you hear a noise? See something, perhaps?'

I shake my head. Lindy had told me to keep it simple. 'Don't go trying to be clever. Don't start to elaborate because that's when you'll trip up. Just say what you saw.'

I wish Lindy were here. No I don't. I never want to see her again. The DS keeps looking at me. I feel myself grow hot under her gaze.

I want to go upstairs, have a shower and change out of these clothes, but I can't face all that blood. Instead, I make my way to the kitchen, Dad's arm around my waist for support. Mum is putting the kettle on. The girls are sitting at the table looking traumatised. I'm glad they haven't been allowed upstairs. I don't want them seeing the blood.

They rush over to me and put their arms around me. Sally starts crying. She keeps saying how much she's going to miss her dad.

Annie just holds me tight, she's never been one to show her emotions. Sally was the melodramatic one of the two. If she broke one of her dolls, it was the end of the world. Annie was more practical. 'Can she be fixed? Can I get a new one, please?'

'Oh, what am I going to do?' Sally wails. 'My dad. Killed! Who would want to hurt him like that?'

'*Our* dad, Sally. He was my dad too,' Annie says quietly.

'I know. I didn't mean it like that.'

I look at Sally and my heart breaks in two. How callous he was. Prepared to destroy her just for a few thousand miserable pounds. For the first time since it happened, it occurs to me that his death might have been justified.

A second DS appears. I pull my girls closer. 'I'm sorry for your loss. A tragic accident indeed.'

An accident? I hold my breath.

'It looks like it was an opportunist. Possibly they'd been following him, your father tried to stop them and it all got out of hand. I'm sorry but you'll have to come to the station to give a statement. When you feel up to it, but the sooner the better.'

My heart sinks. 'What for?'

'It's just procedure, Mrs Hicks.'

'Yes, but what about finding the person who did this?' Sally asks.

I take the cup of tea Mum is offering and hand it to Sally. 'It's all right, Sally. The police know what they're doing.'

Beth has arrived. I can hear her shouting at the reporters outside. 'You're a bunch of fucking parasites the lot of you! Have you no respect? Why don't you leave these people alone?'

She marches in, slamming the door behind her and shutting out the clamour. She studies me closely. I turn away, trying to look as if I'm overwhelmed by grief. The DS, I notice, has two freckles above her left eyebrow, giving her an inquisitive look. She is watching the two of us.

I wonder what Lindy is up to right now. Maybe she's outside, mingling with the pack of reporters, watching what's going on.

On cue, my mobile vibrates in my pocket.

I excuse myself and slip out of the kitchen. The only place I can find where I won't be overheard is the shed in the back garden.

'The police are still here,' I say. I forgot to bring a coat out with me and I'm shivering.

'What have you told them?'

'Nothing of course. Like you said, I kept it simple. Only—'

'What?'

'I might have added a little something, but the officer was fine about it.'

'What did you add?'

I sigh. 'I just said that I felt something was off when I walked into the house.'

'Well, don't elaborate. If they ask, say you don't know why you said that, it must have been the sho—'

'What the hell was that all about?'

Startled, I jump, dropping the phone. 'Beth!'

* * *

The police have finally closed the case. After two months on tenterhooks, I can at last relax. I haven't seen Lindy at all. Every so often she calls me. I don't know what she wants me to do about Frank. We haven't spoken about that night. I haven't wanted to. I don't want her telling me anything that I might let slip later.

She sounds calm. She's still working at the hotel, she says. I keep expecting her to tell me when she wants me to . . . do something about Frank.

In truth, I dread every single one of her calls.

Beth finally tackles me over what she overheard that day in the shed. I knew she would at some point.

Her voice is cold. 'All right, sister dearest. I think enough time has passed now. Why don't you tell me just what the hell you were up to.'

'Forget it, Beth. Some things are best left unsaid.'

'Bullshit, Mia. I know what I heard. You're involved in some way in what happened to Ricky. I know he was knocking you about, you told me so yourself. You've been quite the actress these past months, I must say. The perfect grieving little wife.'

We're in my kitchen. As usual, she's making herself at home, fussing with the coffee machine. She holds up a coffee pod. 'This is the last one. Do you still keep the new ones in the pantry?'

'Wait! No. They're in that cupboard over there.' I don't use the pantry anymore. I've never told Beth that Ricky used to keep me locked up in there.

'There's only you, me and the dogs here now. I want to know what happened with Ricky. From what I heard of your conversation, it's clear you had something to do with his death. Was it you that killed him?'

'Give me some credit, Beth. Why would I do that and risk going to prison?'

She shrugs. 'Okay, so you didn't kill him. But you know who did, don't you?'

'No.' I take a sip of the coffee she's offering. It's good and strong, just how I like it. That's something I've been really enjoying — not having Ricky controlling what I eat and drink. Doing what I want. It's like being reborn. As for Beth, the less she knows, the less she suspects I had a motive for killing him. 'It's just like I said to the police. I came home and found him dead.'

She fixes her gaze on me as if she's trying to tell me something.

'What?' I say.

'You don't have to go through this on your own, you know. I'm not going to give you up to the police. The wanker had it coming and I'm not sorry he's dead, and I don't think you are either. Not after what he did to Stan and Ollie, and the way he abused you. You're safe, Mia. Unburden yourself and tell me.'

'What, you think I hired a hitman to kill him? And for your information, I'm playing the grieving wife for my girls. They are suffering enough as it is. The last thing I want is for them to know what a complete bastard he was — and not just because he gave me a few bruises.'

'Ha! Now we're getting somewhere. So he wasn't just bashing you about, was he? There's more to it.'

'Come on, Beth. You know what he was doing. The affair — remember?'

'No, Mia, I mean something he was doing to you. Something you're keeping to yourself for some reason. I'm your sister. Why won't you trust me?'

I didn't realise she knew me so well. She never seemed to pay me much attention. Clearly I was wrong.

'I didn't do it.'

'It won't look good for you if the police find out you've been keeping information from them.'

I burst into tears. Beth is right. I can't keep this up on my own. I need to tell someone about the pact with Lindy. How scared I am that Lindy is going to ask me to fulfil my part of the bargain by killing her husband. 'Oh, Beth, I'm in such a mess.'

'Tell me, Mia.'

'It was Lindy's idea. She found out that Ricky was abusing me, and I confided in her because there was no one else I could tell. You're right. It's not just the abuse. There's other stuff.'

So I tell her. I tell her how our Uncle Martin raped me. About Sally. About the money, and Ricky's reaction when he found out. She listens in silence.

After I've finished, neither of us says anything for a long time.

Finally, Beth says, 'You have to tell the police.'

'No! No, I won't. I can't do that, it will destroy Dad and Sally. There's no need for them to know about it. It happened a long time ago, and if Ricky hadn't found the letters, none of it would have happened. I thought you said I'd be safe.' I look at her. 'You won't tell the police, will you?'

'Mia, I said I wouldn't, and I won't. But what if they find out? You're an accessory to murder. You'll do time, and then your girls will most definitely be destroyed. And Uncle Martin, of all people. I'll never be able to face him again.

'As for Lindy, she's off her head. Who concocts a plan like that and carries it through? You must see how mad that is. And what are you going to do if — no, *when* she asks you to kill Frank?'

'I won't do it of course.'

Beth laughs. 'But she has a recording of you saying you'll kill Ricky! What's to stop her shopping you to the police if you refuse. Oh my God, I can't believe you've got yourself into such a mess. I wish you'd talked to me before you agreed to this crazy plan.'

'You don't know how scared I was. He had me trapped. You have no idea of the state I was in.' I wish I'd never told her now. Hearing about abuse is not the same as suffering it. I did want to kill Ricky, but I loved him too, mad as that sounds. Not even Beth can understand that.

I'm afraid she'll take it upon herself to do something, believing she's acting for the best. I'm so tired. Tired of waiting for Lindy to tell me to fulfil my part of the bargain. Tired of going over it all in my head. Will it never be over? 'I'm sorry I told you now, it was a mistake. I should have kept quiet.'

'How can I just sit and do nothing knowing that at any moment my sister is going to commit murder?'

This is precisely why I never told anyone about Sally. Granny was right. Never trust anyone with a secret, because it will only come out in the end.

Beth is still trying to reason with me but I've switched off.

I have to speak to Lindy, sooner rather than later. She has to know I will never go through with her plan.

Ricky and I lived a lie. Our marriage was a sham, from start to finish. How could I have continued like that for so long? Why didn't I fight back? I knew how it was going to be, right from the word go, but I turned a blind eye to it. More fool me. Did I really not see what he was capable of — throwing his children under a bus to satisfy his greed. I should be grateful to Lindy for doing us all a favour.

Thanks to Lindy, my family are all safe.

But I can't give her what she wants.

Beth leans forward in her chair. 'What if I go to Lindy and tell her I know what she's planning.'

'No.'

'I have to do something. I can't just stand by and allow you to commit murder. I just can't do it. Look, Mia, you're under stress. You're not thinking straight. You can't really be contemplating such a mad, stupid act.'

Beth gets up and puts her arms around me. 'I'm sorry I accused you of killing Ricky. I was trying to get you to talk to me, that's all. I knew you were hiding something.' She holds me tighter. 'Mia, listen to me.'

'I am.'

'Apart from anything else, I think Dad should know what a bastard his brother is. We don't need to tell Sally. We're your family, we won't condemn you for what happened.'

'No.' I stand up abruptly, shaking her off. 'It will hurt him too much. I won't have him hurt.' She means well but it's not her decision to make. 'What would you have me do? Invite him over and throw it into the conversation? "Oh, by the way, Dad, your beloved brother raped your daughter, and little Sally is actually your niece as well as your granddaughter." It's not up to you to decide what I must do.

'The reason the situation with Ricky got out of hand was because I didn't want them to find out. I haven't gone through all of this only to have my sister tell them on my behalf. If you go behind my back and reveal my secret, I'll never speak to you again, and I mean it.'

'Well, I don't know how you think you're going to fix this mess.'

CHAPTER 27

Lindy

I didn't go to the funeral. I didn't know the family that well, and people would have wondered what I was doing there. I had thought going ahead with my plan would ease my mind. It hasn't. Instead, I've been in turmoil. The worst part is the emotions, all the long-buried feelings it has released.

I embarked on this plan of mine in the belief that hurting someone else — someone who didn't deserve to live — would somehow make my pain disappear. All it did was make it worse. My pain is my own. I can't transfer it to someone else.

When it came to it, I didn't want to kill Ricky. It was only when he spoke so cruelly about his daughter that I saw red. How could a father want to hurt his child for money? I think of my own daughters. I can't bear the weight of their loss.

Frank is suffering just as much as me. I know that now. After it happened, I was so wrapped up in my own misery I couldn't see that he was in pain too. I have two photos of my girls when they were young. They're both in pigtails, smiling at the camera. Gillian's front teeth are missing. I'm afraid that

I might forget what they look like, that their faces will start to fade. I'm afraid that if I stop hurting, they will be gone, along with the pain.

Frank comes in. He sees me holding the photos. He looks exhausted. The pain is wearing him out too. For the first time since it happened, I feel sorry for him. Who am I to decide whether he lives or dies? Who am I to play God? I had no right to kill Ricky, playing judge and jury and condemning him to death. And then carrying out the sentence.

On his way through the room, Frank passes close to where I'm sitting. He glances down and we lock eyes. He's afraid of me, I can see. I reach out and take hold of his hand and he flinches. Gently, I pull him towards me.

Warily, he comes nearer, until we're touching. Slowly, gently, like he's made of gossamer and might float away, I rest my head against his chest.

I loved this man once. I loved him with all my heart. Frank puts his arms around me and rocks me back and forth. I lean against him and he takes my weight. 'I never wanted to hurt you, you know. Not really.'

'Shhh,' he whispers. 'I love you, Lindy. I only wanted to help you. I wanted to ease your pain. I'm sorry. Sorrier than I can ever put into words.'

'I know,' I say softly. 'I understand.' I stroke the side of his face. 'For the first time since that dreadful day, I understand how you feel. I really do.' I desperately want him to believe me. His loss is greater than mine, because he was driving the car. He had to bear the weight of that guilt, alone. To think my suffering is greater than his is selfish and egotistical. I'm ashamed of the way I've behaved towards him. He's stood by me, and all I've done is add to his misery. Who am I to lay the blame at his door when I too am guilty? If I truly hated him that much, I should have left him. But I didn't, not realising that I stayed out of love for him. And in blaming him, I not only lost my beautiful daughters but I lost the one person who could have supported me.

I believed I was alone in my suffering. But we are not islands. We need others. We need to understand that they suffer too. Frank's pain is as raw and exposed as mine. He needs me. We remain that way, holding onto each other, for a long, long time. We have no need of words.

I didn't know these moments were to be some of the last I had with Frank. I had no need to punish him. He is already punishing himself.

Be careful what you wish for.

CHAPTER 28

Lindy

'Hello!' I haven't heard that voice in a long time. I'm having breakfast with Frank in a small coffee shop down one of the side streets in Knutsford. An old jazz song plays quietly in the background. I'm nervous, as if Frank is someone I'm just getting to know. The song is Frank Sinatra's "Accidents Will Happen". How apt. The chatter of the morning customers, the hiss of the coffee machine, all fade into the background as I sit pondering what I've done. I glance at Frank. He looks untroubled. I can never tell him about Ricky, and the terrible thing I did. The two of us are together again, comforting each other as we should have done right from the start. No need to bring any more pain into our lives. I want us to work. I realise how much I've missed my husband, and how lonely I've been without him.

After that first "hello", Mia stands by our table. She looks odd, her face is set in a peculiar expression I've never seen before. She looks tired, older, as if she's aged a decade since Ricky's death. It's been nearly six months. I haven't called, I've kept my distance since the funeral. I should speak to her and tell her of the decision I've come to. But I've been putting it off, waiting until I can find the right words. There are no right words, of course. Frank and I are working it out, we're going to be OK, and I don't want to think about anything else.

Looking up at her, my smile starts to fade. 'Oh, er, hi. How're you doing?'

'Not as well as you, by the looks of it.'

She shoots a look at Frank, and I introduce them. She barely acknowledges him, instead she stares at me, still with that odd, set expression. I look away.

Sensing the tension, Frank gets up, saying he's going to get more coffee. After he's gone, Mia takes his seat.

At last, I think, I can tell her about my change of heart. She'll be pleased to be absolved from fulfilling her part of the bargain.

I couldn't be more wrong.

Eager to tell her, I dive straight in. 'It's lucky I've seen you. I've been wanting to tell you for ages. You see, I no longer want you to go through with your part of the plan.'

She gives a short, humourless laugh. She's starting to make me nervous. This is a new Mia, one I don't understand. She's not thinking of going to the police, is she? But there's the recording I made declaring her intention of murdering her husband.

Her lip curls. 'Do you have any idea of what you've done?'

'Of course I do, Mia. But did you hear what I said? I'm letting you off the hook. You don't have to . . . do what we agreed. That's great, right?'

She just keeps staring at me, her eyes cold and hard. This is a completely new Mia. 'You think you can just turn around and say, "Sorry, Mia, I've changed my mind. I've destroyed your life by mistake but I've made it up with my husband so now everything's *great*." Jesus. Was it all some game you were playing? You weren't suffering at all, were you? Look at him,' she nods toward Frank, standing at the counter, 'he doesn't look distressed or suicidal, neither of you do.'

'Mia, what the hell are you saying? I didn't lie to you. And Ricky was destroying your life. I got rid of him for you. I *helped* you.'

'I don't believe a word you say! It was all a pack of lies, wasn't it?' I stare at her, shocked. This wasn't what I was expecting. 'Besides, it wasn't your decision to make. And now you turn around and say you've let me off the hook. How bloody generous of you.'

'But, Mia,' I say, 'You didn't want to do it. I don't understand your problem. And I wasn't playing a game. My girls died, and I was suffering. How can you think I wasn't in pain?'

'So,' she sneers, 'what's your latest plan? To blackmail me? Is that it? Use that recording you made? You never were depressed or miserable, don't give me that. I bet you never even had any children. God, I can't believe I fell for your lies.' She grabs my hand, digging her nails into the skin. 'How many others have you duped like this? What do you hope to get out of it? My house? The money that bastard was after? You thought you were onto a good thing when you found out about that, didn't you? Poor little Mia, so trusting.'

Her eyes glitter. The force of her words, the hate in them, has shocked me to the core. Deep inside, I know she has every right to be angry with me. She told me she didn't want to go through with it, and I went ahead anyway. I get that, and I get she'd be angry about that part of it. But Ricky was going to rip her life apart. I did her a favour and I'm asking for nothing in return. A small voice inside my head says it's not that simple. I push it away.

'Do you have any idea what you have done to me?' she says. 'Do you even care?' A single tear leaves her eye and trickles slowly down her cheek. Impatiently, she wipes it away.

'I do, actually. Of course I care. But, Mia, have you forgotten what he did to you, what he was going to do?'

She gives me a look of utter disgust. 'You're a monster. You had no right to make that judgement. I told you not to go through with it.'

'But you wanted it. You wanted that piece of shit out of your life. I have you on record saying as much. Maybe we're both monsters then. You wanted him dead, you know you did.' Heads are beginning to turn in our direction.

'You wangled your way into my life — God, you stalked me, you admitted you did. Then, when you found out about the abuse, you thought you'd hit the jackpot.' Well, yes, that part is true. She brings her face closer. 'I can hear you now: "Oh, Mia, I'll look after you. You have to protect your children, Mia. You can't let him hurt them. Is money that important to you, Mia?" And I fell for it. Hook, line and sinker. You wanted to know what it would take for me to part with the money. And when you decided the time was right, you came up with your famous plan. You kill Ricky and I kill Frank. Win, win, eh? I keep the money and my secret is safe. Only you had other ideas, didn't you?'

'Look, it's true I did want to get rid of Frank then. And yes, I did see you as an easy pick. But nothing more.'

'You're a liar!' She is shouting now. Frank has heard and comes over.

'I think we need to take this outside. Whatever is going on with you two, the whole café will know about it in a minute. Come on.' He takes Mia by the arm and drags her outside, into the rain.

Neither of us notices the weather.

'You wanted it, Mia. You did. You can't deny that.'

'But I changed my bloody mind!' She raises her hand as if to strike me, but Frank is too quick for her and grabs hold of her arm. 'I said I didn't want you to do it, but you decided to go ahead anyway.'

'I couldn't let you go on living with him like that,' I say. 'I was your friend. I still am.'

Frank looks from one to the other of us, bewildered. 'What is all this about? What did you do?'

'I'll explain later,' I tell him.

'Tell him now,' Mia says. 'Go on. Let's see if he thinks what you did was OK.'

'No. I'll tell Frank in my own time. Why are you doing this, Mia? I helped you out. Is it because I've sorted things out with Frank? Is that it? Are you jealous? Is that it? You lost your husband and now you want me to lose mine.'

'What the fuck are you talking about?' Frank says.

'You lied about your pain and loss. Telling me you hated Frank so much you wanted him dead. It was a lie, wasn't it?'

Frank stares at her, then turns his gaze on me. 'What is this? What's she saying?'

'Frank. I will tell you, but not now.'

'Oh no you don't,' he says. 'She just said you wanted me dead. You can't just brush that off.'

'No, I didn't. I mean, it's not like that.'

'Liar,' Mia says. 'It was exactly like that. Worse. She asked me to kill you. That's what we're arguing about.'

He drops her hand. 'You're shitting me. You asked her to *kill* me? You think I killed our girls, don't you, Lindy! You know I wasn't over the limit. They tested me. I was *not* over the fucking limit. That bastard truck driver was on his fucking phone. He killed our girls, not me.'

'No, look, Frank, it's all mixed up. I will explain it to you. Let's get out of here. Don't you see she's trying to hurt me.' But I remember now. They did tell me that. I knew he had been tested. I chose to forget.

'I can understand you were in pain. I get that you needed someone to blame, but to ask this woman to kill me — that's just insane!'

'Frank, please—'

'I've had it with you. I tried, but I'm not taking any more of your shit.'

He turns and walks away.

'Happy now?' I say to Mia. 'Got what you wanted? At the end of the day you have your girls, and Sally will never know your secret—'

She slaps my face so hard I stumble backwards. 'You're a fucking monster, Lindy Villas. And you know what the worst thing is? You don't even see that you're wrong, that you always have been. Maybe your girls are better off where they are. Dead.'

CHAPTER 29

Mia

Blind with fury, I head up the street on foot, leaving my car parked up. I'm too shaken to drive.

I keep going back to that fatal day. I told her not to kill Ricky, but she went right ahead and did it anyway.

Now I've made the whole thing worse. I didn't mean to say her girls were better off dead. It's not that I miss Ricky, or wish he were still alive. He behaved like a bastard towards me for most of my married life. He abused me. He made me lie to my family and my children. Our life together was a farce. When times were good, I thought he might have changed and that we could be a proper family. Those times never lasted very long.

I find myself pulling up in front of my house. At some point I must have gone back to fetch my car. I can't remember doing so.

It was cruel of me to say that hateful thing about her girls. Before the words had even left my mouth I knew I'd gone too far. She stood glaring at me for a moment, and then her expression changed. Her eyes narrowed. 'Okay, Mia, if that's the way it is, you can give the money to me. I want what you were going to give Ricky, and if you refuse, I'll tell your girls about Martin.'

'Don't you threaten me.' I'd wanted to back down but by then we'd gone too far. 'If you come near me again, Lindy Villas, I swear I will kill you.'

'You shouldn't have said that to Frank. And as for your hateful remark about my girls . . .' She shook her head. 'But oh no, poor little Mia feels hard done by, so she decides to wreck my life. As if I haven't been through enough! Frank and I were going to give it another go, but you had to come along and smash it all to bits. And then, just to twist the knife in, you say *that*. That's what I can't forgive.'

CHAPTER 30

Lindy

Mia has transformed into a real kick-ass bitch. Despite myself I can't help feeling a sort of respect for her. She's no longer the feeble pushover I first met.

We stand facing each other in the driving rain, like sheriff and outlaw in some cheesy Western. I watch her turn over my words in her mind. 'You shouldn't have told Frank. You shouldn't have said that about my girls. You've ruined my one chance at a better life, and I want payback. I want the money you were going to give Sally. All I want now is money. You've taken the rest.'

'Payback, you say. Now you listen to me,' she says. 'I'm going to leave now. You are not going to follow me or try and contact me in any way. If you do, I will go to the police and tell them what you have done.' She fishes in her pocket and pulls out her phone. 'You can guess what I'm going to say next, I'm sure. Tit for tat, eh?' She turns on her heels and marches away. The meek kitten has grown into a ferocious tiger.

* * *

I watched her disappear and then I headed home. I hoped Frank might be there. The house was empty. Trashed. All his possessions were gone. With a jolt, I realise I really am alone now. Frank has gone. All because that stupid bitch couldn't keep her mouth shut.

At around six that evening, Mia calls from her landline.

She wants to talk, she says. She's sorry she said what she did and is willing to send me the money. First, though, she wants us to go to her house so we can straighten things out. Us? Frank's gone, and why should she want him to go anyway?

She's probably thought it through. And realises it's not worth it.

I suspect she was bluffing about recording what I said. I don't think she's smart enough to have thought of it, and anyway, it all happened too fast. She's up to something, though.

But what? She knows I have the recording of her, that I know her secret.

I never really wanted her bloody money. It was just what she said about my girls. I wanted to hit back.

All right, I'll go round and we'll have our talk. I'll tell her I don't want her money, that I'll forgive what she said. I'll tell her we should forget what happened and move on.

Slowly, I put on my coat and head for the front door. I'll tell her exactly what happened with Ricky and how it was that he died. I should have told her long ago.

Pulling the door closed behind me, I walk to my car. And stop. Frank is sitting on the low garden wall, his suitcase at his feet. It's stopped raining but his hair is damp.

'I thought you'd left me.'

He nods. 'But I came back.'

'So I see. I thought you hated me.'

'I did. But I found I still love you too. Running away isn't going to help either of us get over what happened.' He stares into the distance. 'Everything changed so utterly that night. And ever since, I've been stuck in the same place. Meanwhile, the world has moved on, leaving me behind.'

'I know. I feel the same way.'

'Is that why you wouldn't speak to me? Because you thought I'd . . . killed our girls?'

'Yes,' I whisper. 'I needed to blame someone, and you were right there.'

'You went so cold and distant, Lindy. I couldn't reach you.'

'I didn't want you to reach me.'

'Because you hated me?'

'Yes, but I hated myself more.'

'Why — what made you change your mind then?' he asks.

I sit down beside him and he listens in silence as it all pours out. I can't stop the tears. Telling him like this makes me see how self-obsessed I was. How I wore my suffering like a badge of honour. It is good to talk, and I say so.

'It's been too long since we talked,' he says gently. He lays his hand on my thigh and gently squeezes my leg.

It's enough. He's back, and we can move forward.

At seven o'clock on the dot, we arrive at Mia's.

CHAPTER 31

Mia

I need to think. Lindy will be coming for me tonight. I know it. My so-called friend. Care about me? In the end she's turned out to be no better than Ricky. Like him, all she wants is my money.

I head for the fridge and get myself a glass of wine. How untidy the house is looking. I like it this way. The place looks lived-in, a far cry from the pristine and sterile film set Ricky thought his home should be like.

I am glad Ricky is no longer in my life, although I didn't want him killed. Why did I put up with his abuse for all that time? I was a good wife and mother, I didn't deserve to be treated like that, no woman does. Why do we stay and submit to their beatings? When he hit me — never anywhere it might show — I would ask him why. He would shrug. 'Because I can.'

At bottom, he resented the fact that I came from a good family. He thought he wasn't good enough, and that one day the world would find out what a fake he was and call him out on it. *Time's up, Ricky my man, you're nothing but a phoney.* Dealing with his insecurities often drove him to depression and he'd drink too much. Then he'd hit me. He hit me because I'd seen how weak he was, and he couldn't bear that.

Hence the designer clothes, the designer lifestyle. He thought these things would make the world accept him. He never did work it out.

I won't let that happen again. No one is going to control me. I shall be independent and strong. You'll see.

She may be mad, but Lindy is no fool. She will have devised some way of getting rid of me. I have to be clever, and second guess her. She's not getting her hands on my money. I won't let her.

Having decided on a plan, I called and invited her and Frank to come over for a talk. I was sorry for what I'd said and wanted to clear the air between us. I told her she could have the money. She'll be suspicious but curious. She'll come. How can she not?

Then I went shopping. At Sainsbury's I bought a few bottles of cooking oil, some bits for a meal and several bottles of wine.

I set the table for three and start to prepare a meal — smoked salmon and salad. Salad dressing in a jug on the table. I put the salmon on plates, together with the simple salad I've thrown together. Glasses for the wine.

Meal sorted, I unplug the internet. I take away the land line and make sure all the windows and doors are locked. The keys are in my pocket.

I stand back and admire the display. As a finishing touch, I light a candle and set it in the middle of the table. Perfect. Next, I dribble a line of cooking oil down the leg of the kitchen table and over to the window seat. I unscrew the door knob on the inside of the kitchen door, take it off and throw it under the curtain. Beth knows Ricky used to lock me in the kitchen, so she will back me up. The knob simply wasn't screwed back in properly — one jerk and it came off, to be lost in the smoke.

The two of them arrive, bang on time. I wasn't sure Frank would be with her after the way he stormed off.

'I expect you're wondering why I've asked you to come round. Now I've had time to think it over, I see I was wrong to say what I did, and I'd like to make it up to you. I've made dinner for the three of us.' I usher them into the dining room and invite them to sit at the table. 'I was stressed out and, well, seeing you both all cosy like that, I couldn't help feeling a bit jealous.' I smile sadly. Lindy eyes me warily. She's smart, she won't be so easily disarmed. So I turn to Frank. 'Frank, I want to apologise. Lindy never really blamed you for the accident, she didn't say you killed the girls, I made that up, to hurt you both.'

CHAPTER 32

Lindy

You might be wondering why I've come to Mia's after the hurtful things she said. Simple curiosity, that's all — oh, and to say sorry for what I said about the money. I never really wanted her stupid money, I just wanted to get back at her. Mia and I have been through a lot together, and I can't forget that.

The wine has already been poured. Mia hands us each a glass and asks us to 'please, sit down.'

'The table looks lovely, Mia,' I say. 'I'm so glad you've had a re-think.'

Mia sits nearest the window, offering Frank and I the chairs opposite her.

She has prepared salmon, knowing it's my favourite. 'You needn't have gone to all this trouble, Mia,' I say. 'A takeaway curry would have been fine.' I take a mouthful, enjoying its salty, rich flavour, and swallow. Then I realise what she's done. She's added milk, soaked the fish in milk, knowing I'm super allergic to it.

Mia watches me over the rim of her wine glass. I cough, struggling to breathe, as my throat and tongue start to swell.

'Oh dear. Gone down the wrong way, has it?' She goes to the kitchen to fetch a glass of water, snatching up my handbag on the way. I just see her shove it into the cupboard under the sink. Speechless, I point to it.

My EpiPen is in that bag.

She rushes back to the table, pushes Frank out of the way and shoves the glass of water under my nose. 'She's choking on something, Frank. Could be a bone. Here, let me do a Heimlich manoeuvre.' She pulls me out of my chair, puts both arms under my breasts and jerks me upwards, viciously. I struggle to fight her off, gasping for breath.

'Where's her bag?' Frank bellows. 'Where's her fucking bag? She's having an allergic reaction.' He turns to me. 'Where did you put your bag, Lindy?' I try to point but Mia is still holding onto me and I can't raise my arm.

'Did she bring it in with her?' Mia asks, making as if to look around. Choking and gasping, I escape from her hold and stumble into the kitchen.

'Frank!' Mia yells. 'Quick, grab her. Put her in the recovery position and keep her still. I'll ring for an ambulance.'

They lay me down on the kitchen floor.

'I'll call them on my mobile,' Frank says. 'Shit. There's no signal in here. I need to find her bag. It has her EpiPen in it. She'll die without that.' I'm still struggling, gasping for air, but Mia has me pinned down.

'There's no signal here and the internet is down. Keep her still, Frank, it's the best thing for her until I find her bag. Don't let her move. I'll check in your car. You stay with her. Keep her calm.'

As she gets to her feet, she looks down on me with an icy calm that makes me shudder. She's going to let me die. I make a grab for her leg.

'Let go, Lindy, I need to get help.' She kicks my hand away, races to the cupboard, grabs the bag and is out, slamming the door behind her. Passing through the dining room, she collides with the table, sending the salad oil flying and knocking over the candle. Then she's gone, my bag under her arm.

I can feel the veins in my neck bulging, about to explode. I try to tell Frank what she's done but I can't get the words out. My throat is closing up.

'Hold on, Lindy. Mia's gone for help,' Frank says.

That's when I see the flames. I paw at him. Pointing. Before we know it, the kitchen is alight.

Frank picks me up and makes for the kitchen door.

The door knob is missing. Only the pin sticks out. He's unable to turn it. Putting me down, he flings himself at the window.

Locked.

The keys are nowhere to be found.

He casts about wildly for a chair and throws it at the window.

CHAPTER 33

Mia

I stand by the front door, listening to Frank screaming my name.

'Mia! Mia! Help!'

I listen, waiting until all the sounds stop. It doesn't take long, the smoke will have got them before the flames do. I plug the phone back in and dial 999.

'Which service, please?'

'Fire and ambulance. Quick.' To give my voice the right note of desperation, I picture my girls in that kitchen. It does the trick, there are real tears in my eyes. 'We were having a meal . . . She had some sort of reaction and . . . she couldn't breathe. She was lashing about. I ran to the car to get her handbag with her EpiPen in it and when I got back the kitchen door was closed. I couldn't open it! Oh God, I couldn't save them!'

'You said there's a fire,' the operator says. 'Listen. You need to stay calm and leave the house immediately. Get your-self to safety.' Having dropped Lindy's bag in the footwell of her car, I am well out of reach of danger. No fear of that. 'The fire and ambulance service are on their way. Are you away from the building?'

'Yes,' I sob.

'Whatever you do, you must not go back into the building. Do you understand?'

'I had candles lit. They must have knocked them over. God, it's my fault. I shouldn't have lit the candles. Hurry! You need to hurry.' I end the call before I overdo my performance.

I stand at the end of my drive listening for the sirens.

When the emergency services arrive, I tell them they're in the kitchen. They sit me in the back of an ambulance, wrapped in a foil blanket to keep me from going into shock. No fear of that happening.

They find the two of them lying on the floor, dead. They don't say if they are asphyxiated. Or burnt. In any case, they're dead.

I am quite proud of my performance. Especially my guilt on finding I couldn't get them out.

I wait until the fire is out, and then I call Beth and the girls, who arrive looking distraught. The house hasn't burned down completely, only enough to make it unsafe. The fire service tells me it will need knocking down.

Unable to take my eyes off the wreckage, I regard my handiwork. It is a clear night, full of stars. If Lindy is watching from up there somewhere, I know just what she'll say.

Well, Mia, I knew you were up to something. Only I never thought you'd kill me. Tut tut, Mia, I help you out of a bad situation, and this is how you repay me.'

I shiver. I tell myself Lindy never wanted to be my friend anyway. Like all the rest of them, she only wanted my money.

It'll be all over the media by tomorrow. People love a good tragedy. It will sell a lot of papers. My tragedy is old news. *The young couple who once had it all, only to lose it all in the end.* That's a good strapline.

People will gossip about Lindy and Frank for a while. "They were very private, you know. You didn't often see them together. They always looked sad. He was scary, I wouldn't let my children near him. He looked quite bonkers."

It will take me a while to "get over my shock". Then, when I feel it is safe to do so, I'll take up my life again.

The police will question me, of course. 'How well did you know them?'

'Not very well really, Officer. They kept themselves to themselves. There was some tragedy — they lost their two daughters in an accident. She befriended me after my husband died.'

'How did you meet?'

'She worked at the hotel. She always looked sad. I caught her crying in the ladies once, and I reached out to her.'

'Do you know anything about her family in the States?'

'No.'

'We believe they both used to be architects, is that right?'

'I think she mentioned something like that.'

Once I get the insurance money for the house, I'll be moving. Devon has always appealed to me. It's just far enough away.

* * *

So there you have it, the story of two women desperate to change their lives, and their unlikely friendship.

Friendship can be dangerous.

Be careful who you trust.

I am no longer the woman I was when my story began. Lindy thought she was doing me a favour by releasing me from my part of the bargain. She believed I wasn't capable of murder. How wrong she was. I am stronger than she knew. Stronger than anyone will ever know. I have the courage to change the things I can, and the understanding that fate will change those I cannot.

I'm glad my house burned down. It freed me from the memories of the dark days with Ricky. The letter has gone too. Nobody will learn my secret, and Sally is safe.

I may tell her one day, who knows?

I will prosper because I am strong. Sometimes we have to walk to the very edge of the cliff to realise there's more than one way to pull back from the brink.

THE END

THE CHOC LIT STORY

Established in 2009, Choc Lit is an independent, award-winning publisher dedicated to creating a delicious selection of quality women's fiction.

We have won 18 awards, including Publisher of the Year and the Romantic Novel of the Year, and have been shortlisted for countless others. In 2023, we were shortlisted for Publisher of the Year by the Romantic Novelists' Association.

All our novels are selected by genuine readers. We are proud to publish talented first-time authors, as well as established writers whose books we love introducing to a new generation of readers.

In 2023, we became a Joffe Books company. Best known for publishing a wide range of commercial fiction, Joffe Books has its roots in women's fiction. Today it is one of the largest independent publishers in the UK.

We love to hear from you, so please email us about absolutely anything bookish at choc-lit@joffebooks.com

If you want to hear about all our bargain new releases, join our mailing list: www.choc-lit.com/contact

www.ingramcontent.com/pod-product-compliance
Ingram Content Group UK Ltd.
Pitfield, Milton Keynes, MK11 3LW, UK
UKHW040321161224
452405UK00010B/32